The Haunting of Sam Cabot

By Mark Edward Hall

Apocalypse Island

Soul Thief

Song of Ariel

The Children in the Lake

Moonfire

Blue Light Series (Three Complete Novels)

The Lost Village

The Haunting of Sam Cabot

The Holocaust Opera

Servants of Darkness

The Fear

The Hero of Elm Street

The Sun God

Haunted Tales

The Haunting of Sam Cabot

Mark Edward Hall

Lost Village Publishing

This book is dedicated to Sheila, who wanted the old house as much as I did.

The Haunting of Sam Cabot

Mark Edward Hall

Prologue

Daddy . . . Daddy . . . won't you come down here and play with me? Please, Daddy, it's so lonely here.

The voice echoes up through the passages of time, and along with it, another voice.

"Yes, son," I hear myself say, nearly stumbling in my haste to locate the source of the voice. "I'm coming. But where are you?"

Down here in the dark.

I stop and close my burning eyes, my body trembling. I know it isn't him. How can it be?

I've been here before, of course, many times, but only in nightmares. Coming back for real had not been an easy decision. All roads may lead to Rome, as the saying goes—all roads do not, however, lead to the town of Davenport, Maine. After ten years, I had come to the realization that, as a road can carry one away, so again it can carry one back.

I stumble toward the rim of the cellar hole and stare down into the water-filled pit, trying to see into its murky depths. Something shifts down there causing a ripple on the surface, like a large fish coming up for bait. I flinch, frightened that what I am seeing might actually be real. Then it is gone and I cannot say with any certainty that I'd seen anything at all.

I back away from the rim a little and let my breathing settle down.

A lot has happened in those years since leaving this place; success beyond my wildest expectations; four best-selling novels; admiration from legions of fans. Isn't that what every writer wants? Isn't that what every writer dreams about? Of course it is, but . . . at what cost?

Now the same old doubts and fears, the same horrors I thought I had become immune to cling to me just as surely as tendrils of morning fog cling like silken ghosts to the ruins of this place I had once called home.

Traffic murmurs in the distance. A new highway was recently built across town, and its incessant whisperings are like voices from the past, succeeding only in unnerving me.

I advance a few yards along the wet walkway. Toward the back of the foundation, a child's shoe, blackened by fire, and twisted like seared flesh, lays half in, half out of a murky puddle. A gold-plated picture frame that once held a long-lost photograph—perhaps her photograph—lays burnt and misshapen in a thicket of tangled weeds.

Someone once wrote that terror is most probably life's purest emotion. If that is so, then grief is its most debilitating. I can no longer deny its hold on me. I wipe the tears away with the sleeve of my overcoat, not wanting to accept their intimations.

The distant highway's whispering ceases momentarily only to be followed by a silence so profound it is almost unnerving. I hold my breath and the silence is complete.

This old granite-lined hole in the ground does not, in itself, seem like such a terrifying place. A curious pedestrian might be intrigued merely by remnants of ruin, as people in all of their incomprehensible complexity sometimes are. I suppose that over the years a host of errant curiosity seekers must have visited this site. It is easy to imagine children playing here, tossing stones into the water-filled pit, innocently unaware of the malevolence that might still be lurking somewhere beneath that gloomy surface.

I continue along the path and stop at a place where the trail clings much closer to the rim of the cellar hole. Again I peer down into its dark heart, both hoping and terrified that I will see something tangible in its depths. Perhaps they *are* still down there, floating in that pool of impenetrable gloom, unseen but seeing. The thought paralyzes me and I am powerless to look away. The ghost of Farnham House rises suddenly up out of the dark, watery depths and becomes whole and substantive before me, and along with its reconstruction comes the flood of memories that I am powerless to stem.

Chapter 1

We bought the old house in Davenport, Maine because it had been cheap. Not that architecture didn't play a role in our decision. It did. We found the best of both worlds. We were lucky. Or so we thought at the time.

I was still trying to hammer out my first novel, an epic work of fiction, based in part on a bizarre incident that occurred when I was a teenager. It wasn't working. Writers block had set in like constipation. I was frustrated, and several times even flirted with the idea of setting a torch to the manuscript. Linda, however, had come to the rescue with cool practicality.

"Don't be ridiculous," she told me. "Why waste two years of hard work? You and I both know that once we're settled in everything will come together for you. What you need is a break, a time for introspection."

She was right, of course, and I knew it. But I also knew that in the immediate future at least, there wouldn't be much time for introspection. We were faced with the prospect of living with Linda's parents during the repair and restoration processes, and I was not looking forward to it. Not that I didn't like Meg and John. I did; I was just afraid that everyone's style would get a little cramped. I knew that writing would become a virtual impossibility, and in some small way, I suppose I was grateful.

Linda and I shared the same romantic notion of what a house should be. *Our* house anyway. So after the stark sterility of most of the architecture we'd encountered in Florida (where we had lived for seven years) the old Carlisle place was like a breath of fresh air.

We arrived there at nine o'clock on an early May morning. The house did not set directly on Farnham Road as I had first imagined. Instead it had its own convoluted driveway—with a tall and somewhat ornate wrought-iron gate at the road. There was an old rusted metal sign attached to the gate that said simply 'Farnham House'. The gate stood open and so I drove through. For nearly half a mile, I wound our minivan through a forest of deep, dark hardwood trees. Toward the end of the drive, the woods gave way to grassy openness as the terrain rose gradually to a grass covered hill. And there atop that hill overlooking the countryside sat the most splendid house I had ever set eyes on. I was speechless and so was Linda. I parked the minivan and we got out, gazing up at it in awe.

We'd answered an ad in a local paper:

FOR SALE, BY OWNER.
OLD HOUSE. CHEAP!
A GREAT FIXER-UPPER.

The advertisement hadn't contained a picture, so I was totally shocked at what stood before us. The place was splendid, amazing, magnificent, all those adjectives, yes, and more, but it was also in the most horrific condition imaginable.

"Oh . . . my . . . God," Linda said, taking my hand and giving it a healthy squeeze. "I think we just found the house of our dreams."

I looked at Linda askance. "You're kidding, right? This place is too far gone."

"No, Sam, look at it. Just step back and see it objectively. See the lines and curves? Think of it as a beautiful woman who just needs a little makeover.

Look at the amazing stature of it. See it with your inner architect's eye."

"I gave up architecture a long time ago."

"You gave up *studying* architecture," she reminded me. "You didn't give up your appreciation of beautiful and interesting buildings."

"No," I confessed, "You're right, I didn't." In that moment I felt a small pang of regret that I'd left Linda in the lurch. True, I wasn't a great architect. I never would be. I'd discovered early on that it wasn't my calling. But Linda was right, I certainly did appreciate the artistry of great buildings. And this one was a masterpiece. Or at least it had been at one time in history. But it wasn't now and it would take a massive amount of work to bring it back. Linda's enthusiasm was contagious, however, and before long I was thinking about how we could turn this sow's ear into a silk purse.

*

Linda and I met at Columbia University. She was studying interior design and I was majoring in architecture. We were both idealists, very much interested in the romanticism of classic buildings. It wasn't long, however, before my interest in becoming an architect had been supplanted by another far greater interest. I had always been a voracious reader, and I had begun flirting with the idea of writing a novel. A friend of mine had recently sold a book to one of the top New York houses and I was jealous. It was easy to imagine myself spending my days hunched over a computer making my living conjuring eloquent sentences. I'd written poetry and short stories in high school but had never attempted anything as grand as an entire book. I told Linda my plans and dropped out of the architectural program with my sights set on creative writing courses.

Unfortunately I ran out of money. Unlike Linda, who had parents with the means to see her through to graduation, both my parents were gone and I had no fallback plan. So I decided to join the Army and continue my education through the G.I. Bill.

I discussed my plans with Linda, who at that time was just a close friend. Or so I thought. My decision to join the army at the onset of the war on terror worried her, however, and it was then that I began to realize there was something more than friendship brewing in our relationship.

The night before I left for army basic training Linda and I spent the night together walking the cold, nearly deserted streets of Manhattan. It was during that week between Christmas and New Years and it felt like we were the only two people left in the world. With a sense of urgency, as though we might never see each other again, we each told the other the entire story of our lives.

We ended the night back at her apartment where we made love until dawn.

It was six months before we saw each other again and by then I was on my way to Afghanistan. It was then that Linda and I made an informed decision to spend the rest of our lives together. We were in love and at the time that was all that mattered.

*

"Oh, Sam," Linda gasped, gazing up at the house. "I don't care what the inside looks like. I want it. I just love it. Please, can't we buy it?" Her question, spoken almost in a whisper begged for a reply in the positive.

I loved it too, almost immediately, despite my initial reservations. Although I knew that Linda would have no problem tackling the interior, no matter the condition, everything about the place screamed for me to walk away and pretend I'd never laid eyes on it. It looked like more work than any one family could possibly wish for. It was a rambling structure that hadn't seen a coat of paint in probably a hundred years. In a multitude of places, old clapboard siding hung loose, flapping in the breeze like so many disembodied pigeon wings. Porches and steps were rotted and falling away. Windows were broken, roofing tiles were missing. A closer inspection proved the problems to be mostly superficial, however; items which could be repaired without affecting the house's character and solid construction. As we found out on that day, the underpinnings were sturdy and free of rot. The foundation was of granite and sound as the Rock of Gibraltar.

"Are we gonna buy it?" Sean asked, looking up at me with big blue eyes. Sean was six at the time, a rambunctious little blond-haired fellow with a wide smile and an innately curious nature.

"I don't know," I told him. "The place sure does need a lot of work."

"We can do it," Linda said. "I know we can. It's just the challenge we've been dreaming about."

The challenge you've *been dreaming about,* I thought but did not voice. Although we had been talking about the possibility of finding a reasonably priced fixer upper, I was more anxious to finish my first novel than to immerse myself in a project that could take the better part of a year to complete.

Sean was staring fixedly toward the house's canted front porch. I looked too, and started when I saw the white-haired man who occupied the shadows there. He was sitting in an old rocking chair staring back at us. I don't know how I'd missed him. I was almost certain he hadn't been there the moment before. There was no car in view, just a shiny red and chrome fat-wheeled bicycle that looked to be nineteen-fifties vintage leaning against one of the skewed porch columns.

I approached the porch. The man sitting there was an odd-looking character. He was lanky and lean, hawk like, his skin pallid, the color of spoiled milk. Despite that, his complexion seemed curiously unlined, as though neither time nor the elements much affected its perfect indifference.

"So . . . you folks just moved up from Florida," was the man's initial greeting.

We'd spoken on the phone the day before and that's what I'd told him. "That's right," I replied. "And you must be Mr. Carlisle."

"Francis to you," he said getting up and extending his hand. "Or just plain Carlisle would be even better. That's what all the locals call me. Never did take much to the idea of answering to Francis. Hate the name. Always have. I think it was my father's idea of a sick joke, if you want the truth." He grunted and gave us a sour little smile.

"Pleased to meet you . . . Carlisle," I said, "We're the Cabots, I'm Sam, this is my wife Linda, and that rambunctious little fellow over there doing somersaults on your lawn is Sean."

"Humph!" Carlisle grunted again. "These days more like a hay-field than a lawn." He was watching Sean carefully and his small pale-blue eyes had sharpened to dazzling pinpoints. "Might not be a good idea for the boy to be playin in it. No tellin what manner of kid-trap might be layin in wait. Place ain't been lived in for nearly forty years, you know. Where you folks stayin, anyways?"

"With my parents," Linda replied. "They live at Davenport Commons. You know the place?"

"Sure," Carlisle replied with another slightly sour expression. "Lived in this town the better part of my life. I keep an eye on what's goin on around these parts, you can be sure of that. Those damned condominiums are springing up everywhere, destroying the pristine beauty of our pleasant little community." His mouth turned up into something that vaguely resembled a smile, or it could have been a sneer. It was hard to tell. The expression seemed to convey equal parts humor and contempt. "Live down near the pier myself. Love the salt air. Good for the lungs." He was still watching Sean.

"Come over here, Sean," Linda called, "Mr. Carlisle said it's not safe to play in that grass."

"Oh, Mommy, do I have to?"

"Yes, this instant."

"Oh, all right," Sean said sulkily. He turned and began making his way back through the tall grass.

"Do I know your folks?" Carlisle asked Linda, his eyes now small blue beads. "I've met a few of the new folks down at the Commons. Good people, for the most part."

"Maybe," replied Linda. "They've lived there for a little over a year now. John and Meg Roberts."

Carlisle's face drew down into a mask of intense concentration; his lips were pressed firmly together, the skin of his brow pulled tightly against the bony architecture of his skull. "Name doesn't ring a bell," he replied finally. "But I'm not surprised. There's lots of them Johnny-come-latelies around here nowadays. Can't expect to know em all."

Linda squinted her eyes in irritation at Carlisle's comment. I'm not sure she appreciated her parents being referred to as Johnny-come-latelies.

Sean began to bellow.

"See, now he's hurt himself," Linda said, looking at me as if it was my fault instead of his own.

"Can't say I didn't warn ya," Carlisle said, and I could have sworn there was a small tone of satisfaction in his voice.

Linda went to Sean. He was standing in the tall grass screeching like a banshee. "He's cut himself," she said, inspecting his knee. "I don't think it's bad, though. Not much blood. Sean, give us a break. It's just a scratch."

"It hurrrrts!"

"I'll get the first aid kit out of the car," I said, and did an about face.

"I think just a Band-Aid would do the trick," came Linda's reply. "There's a box in the glove compartment. There, there," she soothed. "It'll be okay."

As I turned back toward the car my eyes passed over the house and I froze in my tracks. A darkness came over me, a feeling of dread so debilitating I thought my heart might actually stop beating. My breath went shallow as a cold sweat engulfed me. Even now I'm not sure if it was in my mind or if it actually happened, but in that moment the facade of the house melted away, and inside I could see ghostlike people from another time moving about, lots of them going about their business, oblivious to the activity outside. Suddenly all the ghost people burst into flame and began writhing like burning moths. Terror hammered my heart. I blinked my eyes and the vision vanished.

My first thought was panic attack.

Following my experiences in Afghanistan PTSD had come down on me like a vast weight and panic attacks, coupled with an intense sense of paranoia had been pervasive and sometimes debilitating. I'd imagined all sorts of things that weren't real during those attacks. Medication coupled with psychiatric counseling through the Veterans Administration had helped to relegate the attacks to a place that wasn't wholly bothersome. Now, as my heart hammered my ribcage and cold sweat slicked my body, I began to wonder if the stress of moving and searching for a house was getting the better of me. I was also wondering if all of the Afghanistan shit was going to come back on me again. But why would it? My God, I was happy. Linda was happy. Why now? Why here?

Saaam . . .?

Where the hell did that voice come from?

I looked up at the house, at the reflecting sun off the dirty window panes, and for the first time I began to question why fate had led me to this place. I caught myself wondering what secrets waited for me beyond those dark windows.

Welcome home, Sam, We've been waiting for you.

I stood frozen, hearing the voice but totally unable to determine whether it was real or imagined.

It's in your head, you idiot.

"Who are you?" I asked.

"Sam! Who the hell are you talking to?"

That was Linda's voice. No doubt about it.

I realized my trembling hand was over my heart and

Linda was staring at me with concern.

"No one," I said.

"Sam, are you okay?"

"What?"

"Are you okay? Your hand is over your heart."

I looked over at Carlisle and he was staring impassively at me, his cold, impassionate eyes seeming to look directly into my soul. Suddenly my legs began to move. "Yeah, I'm fine," I lied. "Just admiring the house."

"Sam, Sean is hurt. You were on your way to the car, remember? To get a Band-Aid."

"Oh yeah," I said. "Sorry."

At the car, I opened the door with a hand that shook and paused, waiting for my heart to settle down. I turned and saw that Sean had wriggled out of his mother's grasp. His crying ceased abruptly. He'd spied an old rusty red wagon which lay on its side, wheel-less in the tall grass and had begun making a beeline for it. Guess he wasn't hurt that bad. I saw what he was doing and shouted a warning. That was the spell breaker I needed as I flipped open the glove box and grabbed the Band-Aids.

"Not on your life," Linda said, grabbing the boy by the arm and leading him away from the booby-trapped lawn.

I came back from the car and handed the Band-Aid to Linda who looked at me like I had two heads. She tore the strip out and attempted to stick it on Sean's knee.

"Ouch! Ouch! That hurrrrts!" Sean whined, pulling away.

"Your bottom is going to hurt in a minute," Linda said, grabbing his leg and forcing the bandage on.

"There, that wasn't so bad, now was it?"

"I wanta play, Mommy."

Linda rolled her eyes. "You stand right there and don't you move a muscle, or so help me God, you'll be sitting in the car all by yourself."

Sean's mouth curved down into a severe pout.

"Active little feller, ain't he," commented Carlisle. His cold eyes were fixed on Sean as he spoke.

"You don't know the half of it," Linda replied with a rueful shake of the head. Last year he was diagnosed with ADHD. It stands for—"

"I know what it stands for," Carlisle said, cutting Linda off. "Attention Deficit Hyperactivity Disorder. Seems like half the kids in the world have it nowadays, or so the 'experts' would have us believe. Back in my day if a kid acted up he got a switch on his backside. You straightened your act out pronto. Didn't really have a choice. Not like today. Back then you made your own choices. Nowadays you've got expensive doctors and drug companies making up all sorts of ailments so they can sell you new designer drugs and expensive treatments."

"So, you don't believe ADHT is real?" Linda said.

"Not sayin that at all. What I am sayin is kids were dealt with differently back in my day. They weren't coddled and spoiled, made to believe they were special because they were lazy and didn't want to learn or behave. These days everything passes for an ailment. I think it's man's way of justifying his own inadequacies, if you want the truth. Make up an illness and a new drug will soon follow. Or maybe it's the other way around. Call me skeptical. Call me old fashioned. I don't care. That's just the way I see things."

Carlisle didn't know our son. And he didn't know

what we'd been through with him. Just the same, I understood his point of view. Back in his day, the "switch" as he'd called it, was the only help they had. But times had certainly changed. It seemed the world had passed old man Carlisle by.

"I wanta play in the grass," Sean said, this time a little more listlessly. The statement was followed by a big yawn and Linda and I both knew it wouldn't be long before he was napping in the car.

"It's okay, son," I said, tousling the boy's hair. "If we buy the place we'll get that lawn cleaned up and you can play on it all you want."

"Really, Dad?"

"Really."

Sean's blue eyes sparkled through his tears.

Carlisle settled back into his creaking chair. "So," he said, "what made you folks move down to Florida in the first place? I can tell you're from around here cause of the way you talk."

"Actually, we're from Massachusetts," I replied. "But Linda's parents moved here about a year ago and suggested we buy a house near them."

Carlisle glared reproachfully at me. "Massachusetts!" he said with incredulity. "Wouldn't be braggin about it if I was you. Ain't nothin but a welfare state for them minorities nowadays. I suppose it used to be a decent place back in the day. Now it's all suburbs and highways and bad drivers."

I stared speechless at Carlisle, convinced now that confrontation was a way of life for him, and determined that I was not going to take the bait.

Linda and I shot each other unsettled looks. Carlisle sat there looking expectantly at Linda and the lid of his right eye was hitching up and down with what appeared to be a muscle spasm. "Well?" he said inquiringly.

"Well what?" Linda asked, and I could hear just a hint of apprehension in her voice.

"I asked why you moved down to Florida." Carlisle's inquiring look deepened. I could tell Linda wasn't sure where he was going with his line of questioning and to tell you the truth neither was I. Was he just making idle conversation, trying to put us at ease, or was he purposely trying to make us uncomfortable? He was doing a very good job with the latter.

"I landed an interior design job in Palm Beach," Linda said. "We talked about it and thought Florida would be fun. We had this silly notion about what it would be like . . . you know, year-round sunshine and all; but more than that we thought it would be great to get away from icy roads and snow-shoveling and all of the other hassles that go along with living in the northeast in winter. But Florida didn't work for us. I guess we're just dyed-in-the-wool Yankees at heart. We talked about moving back for a full two years before we finally did it."

"Good move," Carlisle said approvingly. "What made you finally decide?"

Linda said, "Oh there were lots of reasons. My father's failing health, for one. At this stage of his life he needs to have his family around him. You see, I'm an only child. He has severe health problems and they have no one else they can turn to in their time of need."

"Ah yes, I see," said Carlisle.

"Besides, my job was going away and there really wasn't any reason for us to stay. Sam can work anywhere, you see."

"Oh? What sort of work do *you* do, Mr. Cabot?" Carlisle asked turning inquisitive eyes on me.

"Well, I'm a novelist, of sorts," I replied.

Carlisle's hooded eyes seemed to retreat into his skull. "Written anything I might have read?"

I blanched with embarrassment at that. "Probably not," I said. "I recently sold a book of short stories, but haven't published a novel yet."

"Well," said Carlisle, "perhaps one day you will, and then I can say I know a *real* novelist."

I swear, there was a barely detectable note of sarcasm in Carlisle's comment. I was used to condescension when it came to my writing, so I ignored it. I was determined not to engage this man.

"That is our hope," Linda said coming to the rescue, and then, being a talented diplomat, she deftly changed the subject. "This is an amazing house, Mr. Carlisle. A far cry from those little stucco cracker-boxes they call houses down in Florida."

Carlisle chuckled at this and to tell you the truth it was kind of a relief. I was hoping the inquisition had ended.

"We wanted something with character," I told him.

"Character you got," said Carlisle gesturing at his house. "A whole shit-load of it. But I reckon it's about all you got. You folks wanna have a look at what you're gettin yourselves into?"

Linda beamed. "We sure do!"

Chapter 2

I believe Linda and I both knew in our hearts even before Carlisle showed us the interior that this old rundown New England gothic-revival house would eventually be home. We both felt it the moment our minivan had broken out of the woods and we'd seen the house staring back at us from the top of that grassy hillock. We were a little scared at the prospect, I don't mind telling you. Actually, terrified would be a better description. But the fear was mixed with a huge amount of excitement.

Money was certainly not in abundance. As I'd told Carlisle, I had recently sold a collection of short stories to a small press publisher, which is extremely difficult for an unknown author. The advance had been pathetic and the royalty rate was almost embarrassing. I had a small periodic income from other short stories and articles which were being published at a semi-regular rate in various publications, and I had a VA disability pension of $1850 a month, but that was it. As Linda had explained to Carlisle, she'd lost the only serious income we had when her interior design job had been cut. We'd decided to move to Maine to be close to Linda's aging parents, and in Maine interior design jobs weren't exactly plentiful. I didn't care anyway. I knew Linda wanted to stay home and raise Sean while I wrote my first novel. I was delighted, although I wasn't even close to finishing that novel. And if we did indeed buy Carlisle's house I resigned myself then that it would be several months before I would even be able to get back at it. But it was okay. It would all be worth it, I told myself. Our own home, my family at my side and a chance to see if I could actually finish that first book.

The future was both exciting and a little daunting.

The house was large, much larger than a family of three actually needed—five big rooms downstairs and six smaller rooms upstairs, with an attic, a large shed, and a basement.

Carlisle showed us through. He had been right about one thing. Character was all we had. The place was a real mess. It was going to take an incredible amount of effort to whip it into livable shape. The second floor was the worst. All the walls had been covered with paper of varying patterns and degrees of color at one time or another. Now most of it had yellowed and was peeling off in large sheets. On the plaster beneath, there were large stains caused by water leakage. All of the ceilings were fragmented with multiple networks of tiny cracks, spreading out and crossing each other like the veins of a leaf. Linda went through, taking it all in with her interior designer eye. I could tell that she was aching to get her hands on the place. Just another challenge to her. No big deal.

It was a bigger deal for me. I suspected almost immediately that the roof needed to be replaced, but I stayed silent about it. I did not want to put any more of a damper on the day than was necessary. We would assess the entire situation rationally before making any decision about buying the place. At least that is what I told myself.

"It was an inn back in the day," Carlisle said conversationally. "Long before my father owned it."

That's when it dawned on me. The gate, the sign. It was all starting to make sense.

"We saw the sign on the gate out front," Linda said. "Farnham House. I like it."

"Named after the original owner who settled here way back in the early eighteenth century," Carlisle said. "Same as the road, which at the time was just a coach road between Boston and Portland. William Farnham was the man's name and he built the inn immediately after arriving. Traffic was starting to heat up in these parts. He saw a need and took advantage of it. They say he was a cantankerous old curmudgeon, but a good innkeeper. Lived to be quite old.

"Of course the place has changed quite a lot since then," Carlisle continued. "Used to be much bigger. A fire sometime in the mid nineteenth century destroyed part of it and the remains were torn off and never rebuilt. The name stuck, though, even after it was no longer an inn. Farnham House." Carlisle paused and heaved a deep sigh. "I guess it'll always be Farnham House."

Carlisle's story sparked the memory of what I thought I'd seen in my moment of panic earlier in the day and I could not stop myself from asking the question. "Did anyone die in the fire?"

Carlisle stopped, turned and glared at me as if I'd said something obscene. "Why do you ask?"

"Just curious," I replied.

Linda was glancing back and forth between me and Carlisle and I could tell she too wanted an answer to my question.

"Can't rightly say," Carlisle said dismissively and I wondered if he was lying. "There's rumors, of course but there are no known records of what sparked the fire or of the consequences of its aftermath. By the time the townsfolk heard about it the fire was long over and the mess had been cleaned up. If anyone died they've been long forgotten." As if this was the final word on the subject, Carlisle turned back around and began walking away from us. A quick unsettled glance passed between Linda and I. Sean was leaning listlessly against her leg and his eyes were unfocused.

We continued on with our tour and discovered there were two bathrooms. One on each floor. The plumbing fixtures, from the style of the nineteen-thirties, were outdated but ornate and beautiful. Linda loved them. The wiring was old and in poor condition. But the kitchen was a large and brightly lit room with lots of windows and nice old hardwood cabinetry that suited Linda's needs perfectly.

"Original kitchen," Carlisle commented. "Imagine it could tell some stories if it could talk."

"So I take it the fire you spoke of wasn't sparked in the kitchen?" I asked, which drew another irritated look from Carlisle.

"If it was, then this wouldn't be the original kitchen, now would it."

"I guess not," I said, feeling like a fool.

"The fire was over there on the other side of what is now the living room." Carlisle pointed. "Probably sparked by a tipped over lamp or something. If you're interested you can even trace the indents of the original foundation just beneath the grass out there. The flagstones are still in the ground."

"Very interesting," I said. A look from Linda told me to drop the subject, so I did.

Each room was dominated by a large fireplace, all in precisely cut granite blocks and in marvelous condition with mantles of marble and huge hand-wrought andirons. There was an old wood cook stove in the kitchen. Carlisle assured us that the chimneys were all in fine shape. The interior woodwork was amazingly ornate. Replacement moldings made with modern tools and materials would cost a fortune. Fortunately all of it was in fine condition and not much replacement would be needed. Things were looking better all the time.

We passed on the attic. Carlisle explained that there was still a lot of old junk and clutter up there that would eventually need to be cleaned out. Linda beamed at this tantalizing bit of information, telling Carlisle that when the time came she would be more than happy to help.

The basement was the last stop of the tour. We exited the house and went in through the outside door. Carlisle explained that the stairs down from the kitchen needed to be shored up before they could be used. The basement floor was earthen and the place stank of mildew and ancient earth. The open door cast a wedge of dusky light only about ten feet in, and beyond that there was nothing but darkness. I could tell Sean didn't like the place, for he shrank against his mother's leg and stared at the dark opening with wide, scared eyes. Linda didn't like it either. She threw me a small unsettled look. Carlisle fumbled around in the darkness for a moment until he located a wall switch and when he flicked it, a single dirty light-bulb, probably of the sixty watt variety, came on, illuminating the area directly over the heating system. Linda and I both gasped, stopping dead in our tracks. I was speechless. One small word came out of Linda and it was spoken in a soft whisper that was filled with awe: *"God . . ."*

*

My heart sank. I could not believe what I was seeing. For all I knew, the heating system could have been a blast furnace used for melting down ore. It really was that big. Along with all the dials, ductwork, and piping, it took up virtually one quarter of the entire basement. Piping ran off the thing and disappeared into the darkness in every direction like the legs of some giant arachnid. On the front of the *Hulk*—as I would come to know and name it—there was a large door, probably two feet tall by four feet wide with louvered vertical iron bands that looked strangely like teeth grinning out of some giant and malevolent maw. In some strange way that I could not explain then, the look of that door, hell, the look of the whole thing, unsettled me. An oil burner now protruded from the center of that strange door, but I understood that this probably hadn't always been the case. This particular heating plant obviously preceded oil-fired systems. It was almost, well, science fiction-looking, like something straight out of a Jules Verne scenario; the main engine for the submarine Nautilus perhaps. But that wasn't the worst of it. The biggest problem was its condition, which was evident even in the dusky glow of that dirty light bulb. It appeared that it had long since deteriorated to the point of collapse, looking tired and defeated, old beyond rehabilitation. I knew right then and there that the cost of a new one would be well beyond our limited budget.

Even so, I was curious. My feet finally came unglued from the floor and I went in closer to do a more thorough inspection of the huge rusty thing. I was shaking my head and frowning severely.

"What's the trouble?" Carlisle asked.

"We love the house," I explained, trying to sound as deferential as I could under the circumstances. "But there's so much that needs to be done already. It's, well

. . . nearly overwhelming. I'm afraid this is the straw that might break the camel's back. A heating system is an expense I hadn't bargained on, and my god, man," I said amazed. "Look at the size of it. Something like that is going to cost a fortune. No," I said finally, giving my head a rueful shake. "I don't see how we would ever be able to afford it."

Linda's heart sank. I could see it in her posture and in the sudden paling of her face.

"Now let's not be too hasty," Carlisle said. "I was gonna tell you after you'd seen it that I'd like to take on the little task of putting a new one in myself. That is, if you folks decide to buy the place."

"*Little* task?" I said amazed.

Carlisle nodded.

"We really appreciate your kindness," I said. "But *installing* something like this is only part of the cost."

"I know that!" Carlisle said crossly. "I didn't just arrive here on planet earth yesterday, you know. I was talkin about buyin it with some of the money you folks pay me for the house, and *then* I was gonna install it. How's that sound?" Carlisle stood there in that semi-dark dungeon of a basement, glaring hopefully at us with those sharp, luminescent blue eyes, his curiously unlined features giving him a strange, almost ghostly cast.

There's something wrong here, my instincts told me with a sudden and irrational certainty. *What happened outside a while ago was just plain weird, and this certainly doesn't feel right either. Actually it feels downright creepy. Take your family and get the hell out of here quick because something damn strange is going on.*

But no way could I obey that inner voice. Christ, I couldn't even move. The silence that followed was palpable; you could have cut it with a knife. I looked at Linda and Linda looked at me, then we both looked back at Carlisle.

I could tell Linda wasn't feeling what I was feeling, nor was she seeing what I thought I was seeing. Yes, she had been initially startled, as was I by the sheer and overwhelming enormity of that thing, but in all reality she knew nothing of the nature of heating systems, nor did she actually think there was anything odd about this one. She just wanted the house. She was blinded by that one single focus. *She wanted the house.* It would be our first home together and she was tired of moving. She wanted to settle down. I couldn't blame her. I wanted to settle down, too. My feelings were irrational. I knew that. It occurred to me in that moment that my mind must be playing tricks on me. My imagination was huge. I suppose that's why I needed to write.

"Oh, Sam," she pleaded, and I was lost. I had never been able to say no to her. I knew I was being foolish and I would think later that there wasn't anything more to my decision to buy the house than the simple fact of those soft, brown, pleading eyes of the woman I loved, staring at me from out of the dimness of that gloomy basement. But I never did totally convince myself of that.

Because there *was* something else to it. Something I buried deep inside me and didn't dig up until it was far too late.

Carlisle was looking expectantly at me, as was Linda. Sean too.

You see, I felt, an *attraction* toward that rusty old heating system.

Welcome home, Sam. We've been waiting for you.

But at the same time, I felt sort of repulsed at the

idea of it.

And these emotions together added up to a confusing sort of ambivalence; a simultaneous attraction toward and repulsion against that great fire-spewing thing that sat dormant, but somehow alive, in the dark mausoleum of Carlisle's basement. And I could see by the look of smug satisfaction on Carlisle's face that he knew it. Linda didn't see it. Her focus was singular. At that moment, she knew only one thing. *She wanted the house.* But me, suddenly I couldn't keep my eyes off it. Nor my hands. Involuntarily my feet began to move and I went over and touched it, tentatively at first, and then I touched it in several other places. I was touching rusty metal, but I was feeling soft, sinuous flesh. God in heaven, I was stroking the wretched thing and Carlisle and Linda were standing there watching me and neither of them said or did anything. When I realized what I was doing, a sudden chill ran up through my arms and into my spine. I grunted involuntarily and pulled my hands back in revulsion, and the two of them just stood there as if nothing at all had happened. I wiped my hands on my jeans, trying like mad to wipe that feeling away.

"I need to get out of here," I said, as I turned and almost stumbled in my haste to exit the basement.

"What's wrong?" Linda asked, taking Sean by the hand and following me out into daylight. "You're as white as a sheet."

"I just needed some air," I said, breathing in harsh rasps.

"I know what's wrong with you," she said suddenly.

"You do?"

"Sure. Your blood sugar's screwed up. You haven't

had anything to eat this morning. You refused to have breakfast with me and Sean, remember? Said you were too nervous to eat. Do you feel hungry?"

"Yeah, I guess a little," I said, but I knew that wasn't it.

Sean was asleep on his feet, leaning against his mother, almost falling over. "Here," I said scooping him up. "I'll put him in the car for a nap."

I took him to the minivan and laid him on the back seat. He was asleep before I turned back to Linda and Carlisle.

Carlisle was staring into the basement. "You know, it's even possible this one ain't beyond hope," he said, speaking of the heating system. "Always did work okay. Just hasn't been used in a lot of years."

I looked narrowly at him. "It's so big," I said. "And rusted." I don't know why I was arguing. I knew the heating plant would be staying. I felt its magnetism even from a distance. It was calling to me, *(Welcome home, Sam)* and I found myself wanting very badly to touch the loathsome thing again. Gooseflesh crawled across my body like a rash.

"Awe, the rust ain't nawthin," said Carlisle. "I'll have her cleaned up in no time at all. You'll see." His eyes glowed with smug satisfaction.

Suddenly, and I swear involuntarily, I turned and ducked back into the basement, leaving Linda standing there bewildered. "Keep an eye on Sean," I told her as I went. "I'll be out in a minute."

"Okay," came the soft, slightly befuddled reply.

Carlisle followed me in, as I suspected he would. I was standing there re-inspecting the Hulk, touching it here and there, gawking wide-eyed, thinking about its size, contemplating its long life and imagining the bodies it had kept warm over the years, and Carlisle said, as if reading my thoughts, "Big house." It was as if this explained everything. "Started out as a wood burning furnace back in the nineteenth century, then during the depression they updated it so that it would burn coal. Converted to oil sometime in the fifties. Now I ain't gonna lie and tell ya it's a corker of a high tech system or anything. Cause you can see with your own eyes that it ain't." His voice was soothing, almost hypnotic. "But I *will* tell ya one thing. It'll heat this old house more efficiently than any of those new-fangled tin-gimmicks they call furnaces nowadays. I know that from experience."

I just gawked and said nothing.

"Tell ya what I'll do," Carlisle went on. "I'll get a couple of my friends out here, experts in the heating business—you know, to have a look at her, see what they think. If we can fix her up, that's the way we'll go, if not, then I told ya, I'll put a new one in. And when Francis Carlisle says he'll do somethin, you can count on him doin it. We'll have you some heat in here before you can say abracadabra, and you can put your money on that, mister."

But it was Carlisle putting *his* money on it, and that made all the difference in the world.

Outside Linda began to scream. I ran from the basement in panic. She was loping toward our minivan which was rolling steadily backward down the sloping driveway toward the woods. Sean was in the front seat sitting behind the steering wheel. I could see his pale, panicked face through the windshield. Somehow he'd managed to get himself up there and had knocked the gearshift out of park and into neutral. Of this I was incontestably certain. I began to run like mad but Linda was closer and there was no hope that I could reach it before she did.

Linda's fleet footedness saved the day. Luckily the grade was only gradual here and the van was not going very fast. Another thirty feet or so and the grade steepened drastically where at the bottom it met the woods which were bordered by an ancient rock fence.

Linda reached the driver's door on a run, yanked it open and threw herself into the moving vehicle at her own peril. In another moment I heard the engine rev and saw the van reverse direction. Presently she was driving past me where she parked kitty corner to the house in a small hollow where there was no chance that it could roll again. She set the parking brake and removed the keys. After hugging Sean she put him back in the rear seat and told him to stay put.

We fell into each other's arms as our hearts hammered against each other's chests in twin staccato rhythms. We both agreed that we'd done a dumb thing by leaving Sean in a vehicle parked on a grade. We vowed never to be that stupid again.

"Active little feller, ain't he," Carlisle commented, not for the first time that day.

Neither Linda nor I bothered to reply.

I should have taken it all as a sign: *Welcome home, Sam. We've been waiting for you;* Carlisle's odd way; the vision of burning bodies writhing in pain; the Hulk and my strange attraction to it; our son's near death experience at the wheel of our minivan. But I didn't. I was too caught up in the house and its myriad wonders to see beyond my own better instincts.

Chapter 3

That afternoon after leaving Farnham House we mulled over the pros and cons of taking on a project of such magnitude. Meg, John, Linda and I all sat around their kitchen table discussing it. They were both enthusiastic, and agreed to help as much as possible. Truth was, they had their daughter and grandson home and I believe they would have said and done anything to keep it that way.

Later in the week, after a bunch of dickering and wrangling, we struck a bargain to buy the house directly from Carlisle. At least temporarily, he would be the mortgage holder. We'd saved enough money for a sizable down payment. We had a local lawyer draw up the papers. At the signing, we gave Carlisle the down payment with a written promise that we would make the mortgage payments directly to him each month until we found ourselves in a position to refinance the loan through a mortgage lender. I would think later that if it had been any other way, we would have turned around, gotten in the car, driven away from that place and never looked back. But I always knew deep in my heart that this was a lie. It had been more than Carlisle's generosity that made us stay. For one thing, it was that disappointed look on Linda's face when I had hedged for a moment when faced with the sheer enormity of tasks we were about to embark on. But even more than that it was that strange mix of emotions I'd felt while inspecting the Hulk, and touching it and stroking it. It was a feeling that somehow mixed excitement with fear, a predilection that caused my head to buzz dizzily and left a dry, metallic taste in my mouth. A feeling I knew down deep, in some primitive part of me—

perhaps the reptilian part that still lies waiting and watchful at the base of every human being's brain— was bad. But I felt powerless in the face of it. I could no more have walked away from that house than I could have put a gun to my own head and pulled the trigger. This was an incontestable truth.

Welcome home, Sam. We've been waiting for you.

*

When I was in Afghanistan the helicopter I was traveling in got hit by a rocket-propelled grenade. We were reinforcement troops on our way to a hot LZ where Taliban forces were engaged in an intense firefight with Army rangers. Word was, casualties were heavy. I was angry because some of the men in that unit were my friends, and I was frightened because nearly every action I'd entered into since coming to Afghanistan had resulted in casualties, sometimes heavy. The laws of chance said that eventually my number would come up.

My number came up big time that day. The chopper never made it to the LZ. Like a trapdoor spider crawling up out of a hole in the ground, a sniper holding a rocket-propelled grenade launcher appeared out of nowhere. Too late for the pilot to take evasive action, the sniper fired his weapon. The grenade slammed through the cabin wall just beneath the instrument panel and exploded killing both pilots instantly. I was sitting on a canvas mesh seat midway back behind the pilot seat just beyond two other soldiers, both my friends. They were both killed. But I wasn't touched. Not a single scratch.

All afire, the Blackhawk helicopter spun and

cartwheeled for several minutes before striking the ground and exploding. I remember vividly those last terrifying moments before we struck. It's one of those things you hope someday you will forget but never quite do. I still wake up occasionally in the night in a cold sweat with the sensation of falling and burning, thinking that these must be the last moments of my life. They weren't, but there have been times since that day that I wish they had been.

I woke up in a field hospital with my left arm in a cast and bandages over a good part of my body being told how lucky I was. My elbow was shattered. They'd installed a pin in it and if all went well I would most probably regain the use of it. I'd been burned but not badly. When the chopper hit the ground, somehow the impact and the explosion together had thrown me clear. No one else had been thrown clear. Just me. I was the only survivor out of ten men. How that happened I will never know. For months afterward the guilt consumed me and nearly destroyed me. The unit chaplain later said that I had survived because God had other plans for me. Easy and convenient answer. One that's used a lot when all other explanations fall short.

I never believed the chaplain, of course. I tend to believe that chance rules the universe and that I was the only survivor because I was in the right place at the right time. Simple as that. The laws of chance had struck again, and again they were in my favor.

When we made the deal to buy Farnham House I caught myself wondering if I had again found myself in the right place at the right time even as this nagging little voice inside me—a voice I should have listened to but ignored—kept telling me that it just might be the other way around.

But we bought the place, regardless of those mixed emotions (which I kept to myself for reasons I can't explain to this day). And I did love it, just as much as Linda, I suppose. Maybe more. There was never a moment of doubt about that. And in time, those initial inner-admonitions passed. And over the next several weeks I would catch myself wondering if the feelings had even been real.

*

The movers deposited our household furnishings in a storage unit on the outskirts of Davenport. John and Meg simply did not have room for us *and* our things.

If it had been left up to me I would have just as soon placed a mattress on the floor of our new/old house and camped out during the restoration. But I was overruled by all. I was browbeaten into submission, nullified by a louder chorus of voices than my own, that we would be much more comfortable sleeping in John and Meg's spare bedroom than a dusty old house in the process of restoration. In the end I relented. They were right, of course. I was just being stubborn.

And we were grateful to Carlisle for taking over the responsibility of the heating system. On that first day he'd said he would use some of the money we gave him for a down payment, and he was true to his word. When I started to protest he told me it was his obligation and that he needed to stay busy anyway. So we relented and gladly left him to the task, feeling indebted to him for such a gracious gift.

"Heaven sakes," he'd said, dismissing our gratitude with a flap of his hand. "Don't fret yourselves over it.

You know as well as I do that I got myself a good deal just by selling this old elephant. Nobody else wanted it except you folks. Christ, I thought I was gonna have to go to the grave with it still on my hands. It was the least I could do."

Linda cried at Carlisle's brief moment of sentimentality. It was the closest he ever came to expressing any in our presence.

Chapter 4

The weeks following the purchase were hectic ones for everyone concerned. We had a chance to inspect the house more thoroughly and a further investigation revealed that the roof needed to be replaced. This was no surprise to me. I'd suspected from that first day after seeing the ceiling and wall damage upstairs that this would be the case. Luckily we caught it before the damage became too severe.

For this task we called a contractor, a local family-owned company called Farrington's Roofing. They were scheduled to arrive two weeks from the following Monday.

In the meantime, we worked like troopers, and through it all we kept this vision in our hearts and minds of the house and what it would look like, what it would *feel* like, when it was finished, when it was finally ours to live in, when it was at last a real home to call our own. And little by little our vision began to take shape. We would arrive early each morning and work until well after dark every night, work until we were giddy with exhaustion.

"Busy, busy, busy," Meg would proclaim gleefully. She was the kind of woman who enjoyed seeing people sweat, as long as the task at hand was a fruitful one. She and John were true to their word, pitching in with whatever tasks we threw their way. Meg with her hands, John, not so much. He was a smart man and his advice was sound, but these days he was physically unable to work. He would sit in his wheelchair on the front porch and watch all the activity with a keen eye and offer guidance where he thought it was needed.

John had been injured severely five years before in

an auto accident on his way home from work. He'd suffered multiple injuries including a broken back, a crushed pelvis and the loss of his left leg from the knee down. His injuries were so extensive it was a miracle he'd survived at all. And on top of everything else, he was now experiencing heart problems. But privately, Meg, as well as Linda and I, thought that John had lost something else in that accident, something much more complicated than a broken back and the use of his leg, something that had caused the beginnings of his heart failure. We believed that he had lost his spirit, and perhaps even his will to live. Pieces of his health were failing fast, things other than the already diagnosed problems. He was drawn and pasty. In two short years, his hair had gone from brown to snow-white, his voice was losing its power and conviction, and he seemed to be drowning in a sea of self-pity. Everyone around him could see it, but John refused to admit it. Perhaps his reluctance to accept this one simple fact was, Meg thought, because he didn't actually care about living anymore, and it made her sad to admit that to herself. Her husband had always been such a vital, active, happy man. But the fact was, John was quietly fading away, and there was little, it seemed, that anybody in this great big world of instant miracles could do about it.

But there was one small spark of hope. A relationship seemed to be brewing. Carlisle was there almost every day—working on that old heating plant— and he and John got to be kind of friendly. Not exactly friends, but friendly in an adversarial sort of way, and Meg, Linda, and I began to feel this small dim hope. The hope that what John had needed all along was a friend. And in Carlisle, we started to see that John had at least the beginnings of one.

One day I noticed the two of them talking and approached the porch.

"Can't understand why you don't just replace the damn thing," John was saying. "Seems to me it'd be cheaper in the long run."

Carlisle had just returned from the hardware store in town and he held a bag of what I at first assumed were parts for his project. As I was staring at the bag to try to get an idea what was in it, I could have sworn the bag shifted, as if it contained something alive. I recoiled, but something I cannot explain to this day made me not ask and not want to see what the bag contained.

"Maybe so," Carlisle said, answering John's comment. "But I'm not convinced of that. That old furnace kept me warm through many a cold winter back in the day, and there's no reason to think it wouldn't continue to do so. Like I told Sam here, I'm not sure I'd trust this house to one of them newfangled things they call furnaces nowadays."

"Well, there are a lot of new technological breakthroughs—"

"Don't trust technology," Carlisle said cutting John off. He glared down at the man. "These new technological marvels you speak of still burn oil or gas, don't they?"

"Well, yes, I believe most of them do, unless you want to get into geothermal or solar."

"Those systems ain't efficient enough in these climes," Carlisle said with a dismissive flap of a hand. "It'd take years to recover the cost. Not hardly worth it in my estimation."

"I believe Carlisle is too far along to turn back

now," I told John. "It looks like that old furnace will be staying."

"I reckon so," John said with a small sigh of defeat. "I'll have to admit, I wheeled on over there yesterday afternoon and had a look at it through the open doorway." John hesitated for a long moment before continuing, and I swear I saw him shiver as if a chill had passed through him. "Couldn't believe my eyes. Mighty fine job you're doing."

"Nice of you to say so," Carlisle replied. "Well, guess I should be gettin back at it. That old furnace ain't waitin for no man."

John reached over and patted the small red and white Coca Cola cooler beside him. I knew he kept it there stocked with beer and soda for those moments when a break and a frosty one were "just plain necessary." as he'd once put it. "What's your hurry, Carlisle? Why don't you take a little breather and settle down for a cold one. You must be all tuckered out after riding that bicycle all the way out here from town. Seems to me that would be a difficult task even for a young man. And we both know you ain't one of them."

"Nope, I ain't," Carlisle replied and you could hear just a note of irritation in his voice. "And I ain't all tuckered out either. Been ridin that bike a lot of years and I know how to pace myself. Could get to town and back again if I had to. Maybe twice. I know when to take a breather and this ain't the time. Thanks for the offer anyway."

"Sure, Carlisle, anytime. You know where the cold ones are if you ever feel a need."

Without replying Carlisle turned and sauntered in his measured and methodical way back in the direction of the open basement door, his right hand fisted tightly around the top of the bag he carried. I stood and watched him go, my eyes involuntarily shifting down to the bag, which gave a couple of frantic lurches, as though it contained a living thing, trapped and desperate to escape. I looked over at John who was watching too.

"You see that, John?"

John turned his head slowly to look at me, his eyes hooded and a little distant. "Nope, don't see a damn thing, Sam. And neither do you."

"What?"

"Sometimes it doesn't pay to voice things you know shouldn't be voiced." He flipped open the lid of the cooler, reached in and drew out an icy brown bottle. "You'll have one with me, won't you?"

I took the beer from his hand, twisted the top off and upended it, gulping down nearly half the bottle, all the while contemplating what John had said about voicing things that shouldn't be voiced. He was right of course, and I knew it. Following my Afghanistan experiences I had voiced plenty of things I should have kept my mouth shut about; things that had succeeded only in getting me far too many visits with far too many shrinks, which ultimately had resulted in a medical discharge from the Army, which in plain English meant 'mentally unfit for duty.'

I should have stayed silent and suffered alone. You see, in the aftermath of that horrible incident I was confused about the things that had actually gone down, and I found myself blabbing about stuff that could not have been real. No way. No how. Not in this world anyway.

So, it was all a big mistake, and I should have just moved on. But I didn't and I paid the price. We're a curious and talkative species. We like to voice the things on our minds, and never consider the consequences of such actions until it's too late.

"Seriously, what do you think, John?" I asked.

It was a long moment before he answered. He was still watching Carlisle's slow retreat. "What do I think of what?"

"Of Carlisle."

"No opinion yet," John said and took a long pull on his beer. "Haven't known him long enough to form one, but I'm working on it." John didn't take his eyes off Carlisle until he'd stepped beyond the dark maw which was the cellar opening. He turned to me then and said, "But I'd watch him, Sam. Yep, if I were you, I'd watch him close. Something ain't right inside that man. It's just a sense, but I learned a long time ago to trust my senses.

Inexplicably, John's words ignited a species of terror inside me, gripping my beating heart with its cold hands, until I felt like gathering up my family and running like mad from this place we had already begun to call home. But I didn't run. I couldn't have even if I'd wanted to. It was already much too late for that.

Chapter 5

While Linda was spackling, painting, and re-papering, I snaked new wiring through the walls, replaced broken window glass, repaired steps and porches, and when that was done I went down to the local rent-all and rented floor sanding equipment. The floors throughout were in surprisingly good shape, mostly wide pumpkin-pine boards which had been painted a multitude of colors over the years. I sanded them all down and re-finished them to their natural beauty.

Through it all, John and Meg were absolute troopers. Having their grandson around was a great delight for both of them, therapeutic for John, and seemed to outweigh whatever inconvenience or burden Linda and I might have imposed on them. Sean spent an awful lot of time with them in those first few weeks.

As it turned out, we only had to stay with them for two months, and my fears were not justified. They were simply wonderful.

*

The work on the house proceeded so well that we made the decision to move in early in August. The heating plant wasn't yet up and running, but Carlisle worked diligently every day on it and assured us that it would be ready by the time cold weather set in. I never actually heard much noise coming from the basement, though, and thought this strange, but Carlisle spent most of his time down there, and after he'd go home at night I would go down and inspect his handiwork.

It appeared that the man was a fine craftsman, and I needn't have worried. The plant began to take on the appearance of something new and vital. Each day a section of ductwork or piping or a series of valves would be either cleaned up to a polished sheen or replaced. I remember thinking that the new parts alone must have cost him a fortune. I caught myself wondering on occasion if John hadn't been right, if it wouldn't have been cheaper to just replace the whole damned thing. But whenever these thoughts intruded I would begin to feel downhearted and despondent, even guilty, and I would go over and stand in front of the Hulk and stare at it for a long time, as if entranced. My hand would involuntarily lift toward it, and before I knew it I'd be stroking its smooth, shiny new chrome surfaces and imagining I was stroking a living thing, and all thoughts of replacing it would vanish from my mind.

On more than one occasion, I offered to give Carlisle a hand with his endeavors. I was more than eager for the experience. I wanted to feel the joints slide together, to experience the smooth union of reconstruction against my living flesh. But Carlisle wouldn't hear of it. He was extremely possessive of that thing, and I began to feel pangs of what can only be described as jealousy. He said it looked like I already had enough to do—which was the truth—and besides, he had dedicated himself to the heating project and he aimed to see it through. He was right of course, but it didn't stop the longing in me. You see, I was wracked with a strange mix of emotions. I was grateful to him for doing the project, but at the same time I was anxious for his work to be done so that I could have the Hulk and its enigmas all to myself.

The Haunting of Sam Cabot

Chapter 6

One day, I found an old well in the field out behind the house. I damn near fell into it. We were relieved that Sean hadn't discovered it first. Blackberry bushes had grown tall and laden with leaves and blossoms and had fallen over it in such a way that it was almost completely disguised. I was on one of my explorations of the property and became curious as to why, in the middle of an otherwise open grassy field, a patch of densely-packed bushes remained.

At first I circumnavigated the patch, peering in to see if there was a reason for their existence. Unable to see beyond a few feet in I decided to push my way toward the center. In doing so I came within inches of stumbling onto the rotten boards that covered the well. I fought to keep my balance, pin-wheeling my arms even as prickly thorns stitched lines of welling blood along my forearms. If I hadn't successfully regained my balance, no doubt I would have broken through the old wooden well cover and fallen twenty-five feet into its depths.

I went back to the house and retrieved a scythe. After clearing away an adequate path through the blackberry bushes I knelt and removed the rotted boards. Stone cobbles made their way down into a dark vertical tunnel to a murky pool at the bottom. I could see the reflection of my own face in that still water, silhouetted against the bright blue sky above me.

Then the reflection changed into something hideous and I recoiled violently, crawling back away from the rim. I crouched there on the edge, trembling, feeling the constriction of my heart. I could not move; I nearly could not breathe. The fear I felt was a physical thing. I'd caught a flicker of something I never wanted to see again, a glimpse of my own face changing into something . . . monstrous.

It's just your imagination, I told myself, as I knelt there breathing in ragged bursts. *Look down again and you'll see that it was nothing.* It took my last ounce of courage to lean over that rim for a second time. I flinched as the reflection came into view. It was my own face that I saw. Not a monster, just a frightened man with a drawn and pallid face.

Then something slithered beneath the water's surface, sending an echo of agitated rings outward from its epicenter. I recoiled again and jumped to my feet on unsteady legs. My mouth stood agape and I was breathing in short, hyperventilating rasps. I backed out of the tangle of blackberry bushes, even as they reached out and snagged my clothing like something alive, wanting to trap me there, wanting to hurl me down into the abyss. As I struggled to break free I was as close to all out panic as I'd ever been in my life.

Finally I did break free, and with my hand over my seizing heart I made my way back to the house where I fell to my knees on the newly mowed lawn and waited for my heart to settle down.

I never wanted to go back out there. Whatever lived in that well, real or imaginary, frightened me worse than anything else in my life ever had. It took a long time for my terror to subside, and even then a sense of unreality began to settle over me. A sense so pervasive that it was then that I began to revisit the fine thread that exists between sanity and madness, and wonder, not for the first time in my life, just how fragile that thread actually was.

*

I vehemently warned Sean to stay away from that section of the yard, and several days later, after my panic had subsided and my senses had returned, I reluctantly went back out there, again with the scythe, and chopped away the remainder of the angry bushes. Then I drove fence stakes into the ground in a ten foot circumference and roped the well off.

For several nights following I lay awake worrying and wondering what I should do. Finally the answer came to me. I went back with a bucket and a rope. I wanted to take a water sample. I do not know why it was important for me to do so, but it was. This time, I stood a good three feet away from the rim and tossed the bucket over the side. I heard it crash against the cobbles on its descent, the splash of contact and the gurgle of water signaling that the bucket was filling. I then began to gingerly hoist the bucket out of the well. A sudden and strong downward tug nearly pulled me off balance. My mind reeled with renewed panic and I nearly let go of the rope. But I held on, waiting, frozen. The tug did not come again and somehow I convinced myself that the bucket had hitched up on one of the jagged cobbles that lined the well's interior. I hauled it the rest of the way out as quickly as I could, hand over hand and almost gagged at the sorry state of the liquid it contained; greenish-yellow and thick, with a smell like rotting eggs. Holding my breath, I poured some of the contents into a Mason jar and quickly capped it. That same day, I sent the sample off to the State health department for testing.

The results came back a week later, and sure enough, the news was bad. The letter stated that there were heavy deposits of toxic sulfur mixed in with dense organic matter that might take weeks to identify. The health department suggested that I not fill the well with anything solid for this could bring the toxins to the surface. Instead, they suggested that I recap it with sturdy oak planking and stay away from it. The letter also stated that sometime in the near future they would send an agent out to personally inspect the well.

I wasn't holding my breath.

Finally, not being able to contain myself, I questioned Carlisle about what I had discovered and showed him the letter. I did not say anything about what I thought I'd seen in the well. At first he seemed angry that I'd contacted the health department without telling him first. I reminded him that we were now the owners of the house and that my primary concern was for the welfare of my family.

After cooling down Carlisle informed me that the well in question had indeed been the inn's original water supply dug probably as early as the eighteenth century. He then told me he'd completely forgotten it was there. It had been capped for at least fifty years because it had gone bad. He offered no explanations as to why it had gone bad and something made me not ask.

He said the house's current water supply was an Artesian well which had been drilled sometime in the sixties. From that source, the water was sweet and delicious. I could attest to that. So, there was nothing more to do but take the health department's advice. I built a sturdy oak platform and covered the well for what I hoped would be the last time.

*

I managed to hide my feelings about everything; the well, the Hulk, Carlisle and the strangeness and mystery that seemed to surround him. At least I hid my feelings from Linda. Or so I thought. John, not so much. Although he was friendly with Carlisle, he was suspicious of the man. I could tell. And he sensed that I was troubled as well. And although I didn't talk about it, he somehow knew what I was doing out in the back field. John was very observant, even a bit clairvoyant, I thought. He seemed to pick up on things most people didn't. The day I finished capping the well he drew the story out of me, and although he didn't judge me, he did suggest I confront Carlisle with what I'd seen.

"I don't know, John. I already asked him why he never mentioned the well. He got angry and said he'd forgotten it was there."

"And you believed him?"

"What choice did I have?"

"Think about it, Sam. That man has been on this property in one way or another since the day he was born. He knows everything there is to know about this place. He knew the well was there. And he probably knows other things."

I gazed suspiciously at John. "What things?"

"Men keep secrets for their own reasons," John said. "Downright lying is a bit more complex and telling." There's always reasons a man lies. Why don't you just go ask him why he wasn't honest about the well?"

I was a little uncomfortable doing it but I was becoming increasingly uncomfortable with our entire situation, so I decided to take John's advice. Later that afternoon I went reluctantly into the basement and stood inspecting the Hulk while Carlisle worked. At first he didn't say anything, just ignored me, but he knew I was there. Finally he stopped work and turned to face me.

"You want to talk about the well, don't you, Sam." It wasn't a question. More a statement of fact.

I wasn't surprised he knew what I was thinking. It seemed he knew everything that was said and done on his property. Funny, there it was again, the feeling that the house and property weren't really ours, that it still belonged to Carlisle in some twisted way and we were just living there, paying him a monthly fee so that we could fix it up for him. The thought made me a little sick in my stomach.

"I suppose I am," I said, answering Carlisle's question.

Carlisle laid down his tool and turned to face me. "John put you up to it?"

"No," I lied and I could see that Carlisle knew I was lying. But I would never voluntarily implicate John in anything when it came to Carlisle. My distrust of the man was increasing daily.

"What's on your mind then?" Carlisle asked. His tone was curt, impatient, as though he was talking to an imbecile.

I felt my face redden as I struggled to maintain control over my emotions. "I saw something in the well," I blurted out finally. "I don't know what it was, but it was alive and . . . I don't know . . . unnatural."

Carlisle took a step toward me, thrusting his face close to mine. "Let there be no confusion about this," he said. His tone was low, firm. "What you think you saw does not exist. It was only an illusion. Are we clear on that?"

"No," I said, "we're not clear. "What I saw *was* real and it frightened the living shit out of me."

"Sam," Carlisle said in a patronizing tone that further infuriated me. "Don't think I haven't looked into your past. I know about the army and the mental breakdown. I know that sometimes folks with similar problems see and hear things that aren't real."

The surge of blood to my head was making me dizzy and sick. I had to sort out my thoughts one at a time in order to make sense of them. "You looked into my past?"

"Didn't you think I would?" Carlisle said, his voice the same measured monotone I'd gotten used to since making his acquaintance. "I know more than you think I do. I know about your parents dying in a car crash when you were twelve years old and how you had a little trouble . . . adjusting."

"You had no right—"

"Now you listen carefully, Sam. I was kind enough to trust you by taking a mortgage on my house. I had to make sure you were the kind of folks who wouldn't just leave me hanging."

Carlisle touched me lightly, stiff fingers against my breastbone, the weight of his authority nearly stopping my heart. I licked my lips, the clear image of what I'd seen in the well that day blurred around the edges as if melting from the outside in. Suddenly my tongue was numb with cold uncertainty. Had I actually seen something in the well? Now I was totally confused, like I'd become confused about the incidents in the aftermath of the helicopter crash that had spared my life. Carlisle's gaze was unrelenting, freezing me in place with its cool authority. I felt a sudden tingle of fear.

"I—I'm sorry," I said, suddenly unsure why I was apologizing. "I just don't know what to make of everything. Things have happened in my life . . . ." I stopped short of a full explanation, certain now that Carlisle knew everything about me.

Carlisle became less threatening then, and in that moment he and I both knew he had won. He stood back, his eyes softening.

"I understand," he said. "You thought you were doing the right thing."

"I only want what's best for my family."

Carlisle sighed and nodded in understanding. "Of course you do. In the end that's what everybody wants, isn't it? Listen to me, Sam; there is nothing here to be afraid of. There is nothing here that will harm your family. I want you to be assured of that. I want you to depend on it. Am I making myself clear?"

I stood like a statue, my brain buzzing. I was now unsure why I had come in here in the first place. I stood back and looked at the Hulk—really looked at it, and everything else was forgotten. What I saw electrified me like nothing else in my life ever had. It was like seeing a work of art. But I suppose that description pales in the face of what I actually saw and felt. I knew it was a machine, but it was a machine that had somehow transcended the mechanical and had rocketed itself into the stratosphere of high art. My knees weakened and my legs almost collapsed. Carlisle was looking at me as if in invitation, his face flush with anticipation. I went in closer to the Hulk and reached my trembling hand out to touch it. On contact, something like a jolt of electricity shot through me and my body convulsed. In that moment I was utterly convinced that the Hulk was neither machine nor work of high art; in that moment I was utterly certain that the Hulk was somehow alive.

Over the course of the next several days the memory of that day would fade from me like a dream, until it was just a fragment of something unpleasant at the center of my psyche.

Chapter 7

The roofing contractors postponed at least three times and I was getting ready to call someone else when, lo and behold, they finally showed up in our yard.

I was very grateful. I wanted to have the work done before we moved in. They were a three-man team, a father and two sons, and they were fast and efficient. It took the three of them only four days to completely strip and re-shingle the entire roof, and this included all five of the gables. I was extremely satisfied with their work and told them so. Afterward, they picked up all of the old junk and carted it away to the dump in a large open trailer.

Other than my strange infatuation with the Hulk and the incident with the well, things had been going along quite smoothly. Linda and Sean seemed happy. I was relatively happy myself. My strange infatuation with the Hulk was something that belonged to me and me alone. It hadn't grown to the point of obsession yet, although I could feel in my heart that the potential was clearly there. *And so what if it did?* I reasoned in a perfectly rational voice. I would deal with that when the time came. Throughout history, men have dealt with strange obsessions—some a lot more twisted than mine—and had managed to get by nicely in the face of them. At least that's how I rationalized it. I never mentioned it to Linda though. I'm not sure she would have understood, or even cared. It was, after all, just a heating system, not another woman. There was no reason for her to be jealous.

As I said, things were going along well, maybe too

well. But the tide was about to turn. You see, it was from the roofer, Greg Farrington that I first began to hear the truth about Farnham house.

The people we encountered in our travels locally to shops, stores and lumber yards had been strangely silent—perhaps even evasive—when it came to Farnham House. So I was shocked—to put it mildly—when Farrington brought it up. Perhaps everyone thought we already knew about the house's reputation and didn't care. We didn't know, but I wish we had. I like to believe it would have made a difference. I'm not so sure now that it would have. In any event, I'd like to have the chance to go back there and do everything over again. Things might have worked out differently and the nightmare that followed might never have occurred.

I didn't have a clue until Farrington approached me on that day. It seemed like a casual excuse for conversation and I'm not sure he meant anything malicious by it.

Farrington was a man in his mid-forties, balding, slightly thick through the middle with a quiet, almost boorish demeanor.

I was out in the front yard when he came over and began to talk. I stood there leaning on my rake as he informed me, in no uncertain terms, that Farnham House did indeed have a reputation.

It was his final day of work on our house. Most everything was packed and ready to go. His two sons had taken the truck and trailer and had hauled the final load of old shingles to the landfill. There were still several ladders leaning against the house and stanchions up on the roof. He explained that when the boys returned they would take the rest of the stuff down and be on their way. He had a few minutes to kill and he thought I might like to hear the story of Farnham House. With a self-conscious little smile, he apologized for not having said anything before, but explained that he and his boys had needed the work and he hadn't wanted to do or say anything that might have jeopardized that.

I was instantly angry at the man, not for the confession, but for the deception, for the cagey, underhanded way he was going about it. I bit back my anger, however. Now that the cat was out of the bag I found myself wanting very badly to hear what this man had to say.

"Thing is," Farrington said. "I've lived around here all my life and you're the first folks I know of to take any real interest in this old place. Locals figured it would fall down long before anyone else would . . . you know . . . take a chance on it."

"A chance?" I said, raising an eyebrow. "What do you mean by that?"

Farrington hesitated. I believe he was having second thoughts about his little confession. Of course by that time I wanted to grab him by the throat and choke the story out of him. It was, after all, he who had started the whole business to begin with. Farrington hesitated still. My anger, which I had managed to conceal quite successfully up until that moment, suddenly turned to irritation and boiled over.

"Mr. Farrington, if you have something to say I wish you would please get on with it. As you can see, I'm a busy man."

Farrington suddenly seemed like someone who was very sorry he'd gotten out of bed that morning. His eyes, which had wandered in his moment of embarrassment, reluctantly drew back to mine. A cloud cut off a slice of the sun and a light breeze picked up, causing the elm leaves above our heads to gossip. "Well, most of it's just talk, you know," the contractor said in a mildly hesitant voice followed by a nervous little smile.

"Talk?" I said.

"Yes, sir. Stories of things that happened here years ago."

"What things?"

"There was a fire back in the nineteenth century, you know."

"Yeah," I said. "The old man told me about that."

"Bet he didn't mention anything about people dying in that fire."

My jaw dropped and I just stood staring open mouthed at Farrington. I was again reminded of what I'd seen—or thought I'd seen, and since dismissed—on that first day here. It was as if the house's facade had melted away and people from some long ago past were inside consumed in flames and writhing like burning insects. "Funny, I asked Carlisle that question and he said he didn't know for sure but there were rumors."

"Well," Farrington said, "I suppose that was the right answer considering there was never any *proof* people died here."

"Why the rumors then?"

"You know how people are. Mysterious old house with an equally mysterious reputation. People like that sort of thing. I don't think anyone knows for sure what happened here that night. The story goes something like this; for some reason someone locked a bunch of people inside and set the place afire. Completely destroyed one whole section of the inn, but the rest of the place survived. By the time the townsfolk heard about it the fire was out and the mess had been cleaned up. Supposedly the owner had so much political influence the fire was never properly investigated."

"So you're saying it was murder."

"If the story is true."

"Was the owner ever implicated?"

"I doubt it."

"Who was he?"

Farrington looked narrowly at me. "A direct descendent of the original owner, William Farnham."

"Really," I said. It was not a question.

"Really."

"That's an interesting story."

"Yes it is, and because of it a lot of folks in these parts believe this place is haunted."

"Half the houses in the goddamned country are haunted," I exploded, unsure if I was angry at Farrington for trying to frighten me with a story that could not be substantiated or at Carlisle for not being totally honest with us. "If you choose to believe that kind of bullshit," I added. "I, for one, don't."

"That ain't all," Farrington said. "Other things have happened here over the years. Things that are a lot truer."

"Such as?"

"Two teenage boys were found murdered in the basement, Mr. Cabot," Farrington said, exhaling the sentence like a pent-up breath. He pointed toward the open cellar door where somewhere within Carlisle was working some sort of magic on a machine that might or might not be a heating system. "That ain't no rumor, nor is it superstition. I believe that's probably the heart of the house's reputation. At least in this modern era."

I stood in stunned silence, unable to speak. When I did finally manage to find my tongue, I said, "Holy shit!"

"Exactly," Farrington replied.

"You mean to tell me that people were murdered in our house and this is the first I've heard of it?"

"Guess it must have slipped the old man's mind," Farrington said with more than a touch of irony in his voice.

"That son-of-a-bitch," I said shocked.

Farrington shrugged, as if to say, well then, there you have it.

"When did it happen?" I asked him. My mind was conjuring visions of sometime in the near past.

"Actually, it's been a while. About seventy years now I think. But that doesn't make it not true and it don't stop folks from being afraid of this place. It was Halloween night 1944. It was assumed that the boys—both of them locals—broke in. That's the only thing the authorities could come up with, although as far as I know they never found a likely point of entry. There wasn't anybody living here at the time. People have lived here only sporadically over the past hundred and fifty years or so, since the fire. The ones that did, rented, but never stayed long. It's been years and years since the place has been occupied. Anyway, there was quite an investigation, but no one ever found out who killed those boys, or why. The authorities figured they probably surprised a squatter. Maybe an escaped con or something. Coincidentally, in that same autumn of 1944 records show that two men escaped from the Maine State Prison in Thomaston. The escape took place one week before the murders. Those two men were never found. The case is still technically open, but I believe it's been years since anybody has looked into it.

"There's those around here who think something . . . supernatural killed those kids, when you consider all the stories and rumors and the fire and all. Personally I don't believe in any of that superstitious mumbo jumbo."

"So, you don't believe in haunted houses?"

"No . . . of course not." Farrington tapped his head. "I think ghosts and haunted houses and all that related crap all reside right here in the ole noggin. People psyche themselves out. They hear stories and get spooked, and well . . . I think that's the real reason no one's ever stayed here for very long."

I nodded and remained thoughtful for a long moment. "How did Carlisle come by the place?" I asked.

"Inherited it from his old man. It's the family home. He grew up here. Carlisle was . . . oh let's see . . . he must have been around eighteen, nineteen at the time of the killings, off in the Merchant Marine then. Second World War. His old man took sick while he was away, a stroke or something, and had to be put in a nursing home. Rumor goes that Carlisle got word that the old man had died, and in them days it'd take weeks for someone to get home from overseas. In the meantime, the house sat empty, and for whatever reason those two boys broke in and got themselves murdered. The old man's housekeeper, a woman by the name of Hattie Dowd, found them in the basement just three days after the old man died. She continued to come out and keep the place cleaned up even after he'd had the stroke, you see. And she kept coming back after he'd died, too, supposedly to clean. Rumor goes that there was something more between the two of them than just employer, employee relationship. Anyway, doesn't matter. They say the bodies of those two boys were butchered. I mean *really* butchered. Dismembered. Their parts were stacked up like cordwood in front of that old furnace like some sort of offering. Must have been something terrible to see. The old lady that found them went totally crazy. Story goes she ran screaming from the house and made it a mile or so down the road before someone came along and picked her up. She was babbling on about blood and body parts, so the driver takes her to the cops. They listened to her story and came out here to investigate. Sure enough, those two boys were just like she said they were, all stacked up pretty as you please in front of that furnace door that looks like a hungry mouth. Old Hattie Dowd was never the same after that. Lost all her marbles and had to be committed to the state mental institution."

"Jesus," I said with a grimace. The anger had gone from me like air from a deflating balloon, replaced by a sense of shock so deep I thought my knees would give out on me. I was stunned and hurt all at the same time. I couldn't believe that old bastard Carlisle had deceived us in this way.

"Carlisle's been trying to sell this place for years," Farrington said. "Locals won't have anything to do with it. There's a whole list down at the police station of other unexplained things over the years in this area. And there are a lot of folks who insist this house is in some way connected."

"Jesus," I said, my mind reeling. My hands felt

clammy and my mouth had gone dry. "What unexplained things?"

"Deaths, disappearances, hauntings. There's even been white lady sightings out on the main road." Farrington chuckled.

"Is this supposed to be funny?"

"No, sorry, Mr. Cabot. My intention is not to alarm you. I mention these things only because I want to emphasize how ridiculous I think they are. Let's face it, every community in America has a white lady. And most have at least one haunted house. I personally don't put much stock in any of it." Farrington paused. As if by magic, he produced a cigarette and a wooden match. He struck the head of the match with a yellowed thumbnail and touched the flame to the end of the cigarette. He inhaled deeply and let the smoke trickle slowly from his nostrils. "I got my own little theory about all this," he said finally. "You see, folks always got to have something to blame everything on otherwise they ain't happy. Makes people feel better if they can lay their hands on the perpetrator, that way they don't have to suspect one of their own."

"So you're saying this house is the perpetrator?"

Farrington flapped his hand in dismissal. "I told you, the place has got a reputation, that's all I know. Imagine others will be telling you the same thing. I wouldn't fret too much about it. Appears you got yourself a fine home here. It's about time somebody took an interest in her. Like I said, I don't believe in any of that supernatural crap. As far as the two murdered teenagers are concerned, I tend to lean more toward the escaped convict theory."

"But why would escaped cons take the time to dismember a couple of adolescent boys when they should have been running for their freedom? It doesn't make sense."

"Evidently those two guys were both in for the duration. Couple of tough career criminals with a history of atrocities; murder, rape, you name it. They were free for the first time in years. Maybe they just wanted to have a little fun."

"Fun?" I said. Truth is I felt like puking.

Farrington smiled and it was chilling in its ferocity. To me it wasn't a smile at all, but a gaping grimace that showed more fear than mirth. In the next second the unsettling expression had passed and Farrington leaned in close, his eyes darting back and forth as if he was making sure no one was listening. He touched his dry lips with his tongue. Leaves continued to gossip overhead. "Those guys are long gone," he whispered. "But the old man's still around."

"What's that supposed to mean?"

Farrington cocked a thumb in the direction of the open cellar doorway. "If I were you I'd keep a close eye on him."

"Why do you say that?"

"Mysterious old duffer. No one actually knows much about him. Just seems to come and go, you know, like a ghost. One minute he's there, and the next, well, he's gone, and most folks just seem to forget about him until he suddenly appears again."

For a long moment I stared silently at Farrington. In truth I didn't know what to say. He was right, of course. I felt the same way about Carlisle. He just seemed to come and go without leaving much residue. I liked it that way. The less needy folks were, the better, as far as I was concerned.

I said no more, and neither did Farrington. There

wasn't much more that needed to be said. The conversation left me decidedly uneasy, however. It would be a lie to tell you otherwise. But it wasn't long before other priorities had taken precedence. I didn't forget what Farrington told me, but neither did I lose any sleep over it. I didn't say anything to Linda about it, though. I'm not sure why I didn't. I suppose in retrospect it was because she was too happy and I was determined not to be the spoiler.

But it was funny, or perhaps not so funny now that I look back on it. From that moment on, every time I went into the basement, my overactive imagination saw those two boys cut up like butcher shop offerings and stacked up in front of the heating system's giant maw. Why? I kept asking myself. Why would anybody do such a thing? But I believe now that I knew the answer to my own question, even then, but didn't want to admit it to myself. The knowledge began to eat at me, and in the weeks that followed I began to feel more and more drawn to that fiery entity, and I was powerless to control those urges.

Chapter 8

I hold many stirring memories of that summer, some fond, some frightening, some satisfying and some horrifying, but the one which stands up tallest in my mind, the one that will live with me forever, was the afternoon I surprised Linda in an upstairs bedroom. It was a moment of intimacy I believe has as much right to be told as any part of this tale.

The afternoon was sunny and languid. Sean was in town shopping with Meg, and Carlisle was on one of his many hardware store runs.

It was the last day of July and Linda had been wallpapering in one of the upstairs bedrooms. She was turned away from me when I found her; she was stretching her arms up over her head smoothing out some lumps which had occurred between the new paper and the wall. I stood watching for a long moment, marveling at her incredible beauty. She was wearing pink shorts and one of my old faded chamois shirts. She had pulled the tails around in front and tied them together in a knot just below her breasts, exposing her midriff. I remember thinking that even in these sexless garments she must still be the sexiest woman alive. She moved like a graceful dancer, unaware of her silent witness. Wisps of shoulder-length blonde hair would cross her mouth and nose as she worked and she would take her hand and brush them back out of her face with more than a hint of innocent, impish provocation. I snuck up from behind and encircled my arms around her bare midriff. She turned, surprised, and our lips met.

"Oh, Sam," she said, delighted and a little bit flushed. "I'm all covered with wallpaper paste, and what if Carlisle comes back?" Her eyes danced.

"What if?" I said, "This is our house now."

Linda giggled. We slid to the floor and she told me how happy she was. I told her how lucky I was. We made love right there on the floor and it was one of those rare times that you measure all the other times against. Warm sunlight slanted through windows and played off our naked bodies. The beating of our hearts, the quickening of our breath; Linda's soft whimper, "Oh, Sam please, yes, I love you."

I shall never forget that time for it *was* one of the best, and . . . sadly, one of the last. From the time of the discovery of the mask, which was not long in coming, Linda's and my relationship deteriorated rapidly.

The few precious weeks that followed were the sweetest of my life. It will always be a baseline that I use to measure personal happiness, and sadly, success, money, everything in my life, since all pales in the face it.

Chapter 9

We moved in as planned and had a house-warming party the following Saturday night. We invited all of the people who had helped us in our endeavors: Carlisle, of course, John and Meg and, as an afterthought, I invited the Farringtons. Although I had not confronted Carlisle with the things Greg Farrington had shared with me about the house's reputation, I was secretly, and a little bit perversely, hoping that it would come out while the two men were together in the same room.

We toasted our new home and good fortune with champagne and settled down for food and conversation. But the Farringtons did not show and it wasn't until 8:30 or so when I overheard Linda talking with her mother that I realized something was wrong.

"Oh, my God," Linda exclaimed. "No I didn't read the morning paper. How on earth did it happen?" Her face had clouded with concern.

"I didn't know you'd invited them, dear," Meg said. "It completely slipped my mind until you mentioned it."

"Yes," Linda replied, all the color now drained from her face. "Yes, we did invite them."

"What's this all about, Meg?" I said, crossing the room.

"Such a shame," she said. "Such a nice man."

"Sad story, isn't it"? Carlisle commented without emotion. "About him dying that way."

"Dying what way?" I asked, perplexed. "What are you talking about? Who died?"

"Why, Greg Farrington," Meg said. "The man who did your roof. He fell off a roof yesterday over in Richmond. It seems he was all alone at the time, nobody there to help him." She pursed her lips and gave her head a sad little shake. "His boys were off on a dump run. When they returned, they found his body."

"Oh, Christ," I said stunned.

"Landed on one of his ladder jacks," John said. "Evidently the damned thing was lying there on the ground with the metal jack part of it sticking straight up. Paper said it impaled him like a sword."

"Killed just like that," Carlisle said, snapping his fingers. "Out like a light. Never knew what hit him."

"Oh, my God," Linda said again, sitting down heavily on the couch and putting her face in her hands. "I think I'm going to be sick. Those poor boys. His poor wife."

I sat down next to her, feeling a mixture of shock and extreme sadness. Farrington's story suddenly leaped out of that secret little place in my psyche—the place reserved for hidden and unpleasant information—and began swimming through my mind in crazy circles. *Had it been coincidence that he'd been killed?* I wondered. *Or was there something more menacing at work here? Of course it was coincidence*, my rational mind answered back. *Just a terrible accident. Nothing more.* But I couldn't convince myself of that. No way. No matter how much I wanted it to be so.

The news of the death put a damper on the party and so it broke up early. After everybody went home, Linda and I went upstairs, but before going to bed we looked in on Sean. We stood for a long time holding each other, silently watching him sleep. A terrible fear went into my heart; I had the strong sense that something in my life had gone slightly askew. I felt like I was teetering on the brink of some unknown precipice. I won't lie to you, I knew it then, even before the mask and all that it foreshadowed. I don't think Linda suspected anything. Not yet anyway. That would come later. Dear, God, yes, it certainly would.

*

I could not sleep. I lay awake staring at the ceiling listening to Linda's soft, rhythmic breathing. Sometime near dawn I slipped out of bed. Dressed only in robe and bedroom slippers I tiptoed downstairs. I hesitated at the cellar door for a long time, fighting the mixed emotions inside me; shame, guilt, exhilaration, like a cheater stealing off into the night to meet his secret lover. It was not the first time I felt I had lost something fundamental in the war on terror, something more than the piece of elbow that had been pulverized by a hot, whirling fragment of shrapnel. Or perhaps I had *found* something over in that terrible no-man's-land, something no man should ever bring home with him. No matter, I knew I was going down into that basement. It wasn't debatable. I'd been there before, and I'd go there again, and again. I *needed* to go there. I needed to look upon the Hulk. I needed to commune with it. I needed to understand.

I opened the door and slipped quietly down the stairs in the dark. The Hulk seemed benign as I approached it. In the dark it was just an aging and sagging lump of sheet steel and cast iron; the one we'd seen on that first day here months ago, a heating plant that had reached the end of its long life and just wanted to be left alone to die. But of course it was no longer a sad and drooping metal monster. When I flipped on that dusty light it came alive in some incomprehensible way. All shiny chrome, stainless steel and whirring valves, a living thing that seemed to burn with a sort of cold inner-fire that I did not have the capacity to resist. For a long time, well into that night, I stood on the earthen floor in that dingy basement with the flats of my hands pressed solidly against the Hulk's iron skin, talking to it in a fevered gibberish that had no meaning. And it spoke back to me in an alien language known only to the Hulk and me and its servants of darkness.

Chapter 10

August slipped through our fingers like magic and was gone before we knew it. Linda and I were so busy that I didn't notice until it was almost too late that she too was slipping away from me. She'd become distant and preoccupied, her moods dark and pensive. One morning I noticed tears in her eyes.

When I tried to speak to her about it, she was uncommunicative, passing it off as nothing more than a bad dream. I knew what bad dreams were all about, I'd been having my share of them. With Linda, I thought perhaps it was something more. I had noticed the bottle of Valium on her bedside table the week before. She had gone to the doctor for what she'd called a routine checkup and the Valium had just appeared there. She'd never said a word to me about it. She had never before used drugs to go to sleep. Twice I pressed her on the subject; both times she avoided it. It was as though she had become afraid of me. Sometimes when I watched her there was accusation, or even fear in her eyes.

I was frightened now of pressing her too hard, for when I searched my mind for a possible answer, my stomach tightened with fear. I did not want to admit that these changes in her could possibly be my fault. I was changing too, and I didn't like what I saw in the mirror. So instead of dealing with it I ignored the changes in us both and in time we grew apart.

*

With Carlisle's work mostly completed, we didn't see him every day any more, but we did see him two or three times a week. He lived in a small apartment near the Davenport pier—or so we were told, never once having laid eyes upon the place. Occasionally throughout that summer, if it was raining or if I was going his way anyway, I would offer him a ride home. He always refused. He said he didn't like cars and most of the time preferred riding his bicycle, which he usually did.

"Keeps the old blood circulatin," he'd stated in his infectious Down-East accent. "If more people rode bicycles there wouldn't be so much heart disease or cholesterol problems. Why, nobody had those kinds of problems when I was a young feller, before everyone had cars."

I couldn't argue with his logic. I imagined that any medical doctor worth his salt would have told me the same thing. Just the same, later I would think that it was unlikely that Carlisle was old enough to boast that nobody had cars when he was a young feller. That would make him much older than what I assumed was his seventy-something years.

Most of the time, though, Carlisle would just simply appear or disappear without explanation. And this had become an accepted given in the Cabot household. It was almost as if he still had some sort of lease on the place, and we supposed that in a way, he did. We would see him early in the morning pumping the pedals of that streamlined 1950s fat-wheeled bicycle up the long graveled driveway from Farnham Road. He would wheel it up to the shed, lean it against a corner post without using the kickstand, go about his business, and sometime later in the day, he and that improbable old bike would just simply disappear. On many occasions, an entire day would go by without our paths crossing even once.

And when they did cross, and we would speak, it was almost as if the things he had to say were somehow forced, as if he might have been happier to just be left alone to his tasks. I got the feeling that whatever thoughts passed behind those eyes were his alone, secret somehow.

So it came as no small surprise the day Carlisle did finally accept a ride to town. One morning late in the month, we awoke to a light rain falling and I was amazed to see Carlisle pumping the pedals of that old bicycle up the drive toward the shed. What could possibly be so important here that he would chance catching a cold or possibly even pneumonia? By noon it was raining in torrents accompanied by a fierce northeast wind. The weather report said we were in for the season's first nor'easter. The thought crossed my mind that a bicycle ride four miles back to town would be sheer insanity for a man his age.

In the late afternoon, Linda decided to take Sean and go to town for a visit with her mom and dad and then go to the grocery store. I tried to talk her out of it, but she would not be swayed. In the end I relented, but uneasily, cautioning her to be extra careful.

As a polite afterthought—and pretty darned sure he would not accept—Linda offered to give Carlisle a ride home. At first, he was hesitant, and then to our great astonishment, he actually accepted the invitation. I was flabbergasted. All the times I'd offered he'd refused and now he had agreed to ride with Linda and Sean. Wonders would never cease.

Although I was nervous about Linda driving in the storm, part of me was a little bit delighted, if you want the truth. I would be alone for the first time since I couldn't remember when, and although improvements to the room that would become my office weren't complete and I hadn't yet set up my computer, the thought of curling up on the couch with a pad of paper and several newly-sharpened pencils while the storm raged outside was appealing. Some ideas had been forming as I'd worked on the house, and I thought it would be a welcome opportunity to flesh them out. I worked for several hours until the house began to darken with the coming of night, and in the midst of a thought, I fell asleep and dreamed.

Chapter 11

I stood in the center of a vast, dimly-lit room. At first it looked like the living room of my parent's home. It had the same furniture, but the room was much larger than I remembered. And there were other problems. Everything in the room seemed to glow with a faint, blue luminescence as did the gauzy shadows that stretched at odd angles across the carpeted floor.

The first thing that made me realize it was a dream was the way the shadows all seemed to converge in the middle of the room. This was not how things in the conscious world worked.

The second thing that tipped me off was that at the far end of the room, draped either in rotting lace or a clotted tangle of spider webs, two side-by-side coffins lay; one for my mother, and one for my father. Although I somehow knew that the coffins contained my parents I also knew this wasn't at all how things happened all those years ago. They hadn't been shown at home, as this dream suggested, they'd been shown at the funeral parlor downtown.

So, why was I dreaming about my parent's funeral at all? I hadn't dreamed about them, or even thought about them for a very long time. Actually I'd spent the last thirty plus years trying to forget about them. "Forgetting makes the pain go away," a shrink once told me. "Ah, but as much as we would like to forget, we never really do."

Maybe not, but I'd been doing one hell of a job forgetting up till then. And by the way, what the hell was this dream doing in my head anyway? The last thing I remembered I was writing a story about being down in the basement talking to the Hulk . . . *no, that can't be right. You can't talk to a furnace. Not in the real world at least. Furnaces are inanimate objects. They are a collage of iron and tin and ceramics, all dreamed up and put together by the most intelligent species on the planet.* But this isn't the real world anymore. The thought occurred to me that I'd left the real world behind when I moved into Farnham House.

It's not really a furnace, you know. It's something alive. You even gave it a name.

That doesn't mean it's alive. Lots of people give inanimate objects names; boats, planes, cars. Some men even name their dicks.

But this isn't your dick, is it, old buddy. This is the monster that lives in your basement, not the one that lives in your pants. The monster you named the Hulk.

So, what's your point? My problem is I'm dreaming about something I never wanted to be reminded of . . . the deaths of my parents. Why do you suppose that is?

When no answer was forthcoming I stepped closer to the twin coffins and peered down into them, one, and then the other. Both my parents lay on their backs, hands folded serenely across their chests. Their eyes were wide open and staring, like wet glass marbles that reflected the eerie blue glow of the room. Dad's thin lips were peeled back, exposing his teeth in a frightening grimace, not unlike Greg Farrington's frightening and fear-filled grin on the day he volunteered information about our new/old house—information I never shared with Linda, by the way—and warned me about Carlisle. As if I needed any warning. Now, old information sam-overload Greg was pushing up daisies in the local cemetery and here I was dreaming about a time and place best left forgotten.

As I stood between the rotted lace-draped coffins

staring down at the corpses of my parents amongst the folds of satin lining, I noticed a curious thing. There was something dark leaking from their bodies, spreading out and staining the lining. *Must be blood.* The thought shot a quick spasm of panic into my heart. How could it be blood? The mortician would have drained all the blood from their bodies—all the blood that hadn't been lost in the accident, at least—and replaced it with formaldehyde, the standard-practice embalming fluid.

For what seemed like a terribly long time, I just stood there between those two coffins, hardly able to breathe. As I stared down at my dead parents I thought that except for their faces with the open glassy eyes, they could be sleeping. I expected at any moment to see them sit up and tell me what a brave little guy I was for handling their deaths with such poise and sophistication.

But they didn't do that. No, not for a minute did they do that. Even so, I wanted to scream at them, '*I was in shock! What the hell else was I supposed to do, throw a temper tantrum? Dad, you were drunk. You killed yourself and my mother, not to mention the people in that other car. You did a stupid thing. You left me, and I had to grow up fast. There wasn't anybody else who could or would take care of me.*'

Suddenly a low, dull thumping sound filled my ears causing me to flinch with each beat.

I wasn't sure whether the sound originated outside the house or inside it, but the longer I listened to it, the louder it became until it pulsed like a frantic heartbeat inside my head.

At least now I *know* I'm dreaming, my disengaged yet rational mind said. So, why can't I make myself wake up?

The thought sent a sudden rush of alarm through me. Maybe I'd never wake up from this nightmare. I heard myself moan softly, and tried again to come awake. To no avail. In a slow, fluid motion, I felt myself turn around. My eyes widened, and as I tried to pierce through the shadows, I vaguely sensed motion in the darkness. But I couldn't focus clearly enough on anything to know what was there.

Once again I glanced down at my dead parents. Dad was still lying on his back staring straight up, but now Mom lay in a fetal position, her knees pulled up to her chest. She was turned away from me and I noticed for the first time that she was wearing a dark-colored dress that looked like a ball gown—the gown she was wearing that night—which appeared to be ripped and stained. It hung in loose tatters from her shoulders.

No way was she buried in that dress.

It was New Year's Eve. They'd been to a party . . . and, on the way home . . . No, I don't want to think about that anymore.

As I watched, the deepening shadows of the room bled like ink stains into the coffin, obscuring my dead parents.

I felt compelled to move closer to make sure they were still there, to make sure they were all right.

Of course they're not all right, you idiot. They're dead . . . They got all mangled up in that car crash. No one could have gotten out of that alive.

But the insistent thumping sound—that I suddenly realized was not inside my head—made me turn away. *Please let me wake up from this nightmare.*

The sound gradually shifted from a thumping heartbeat to a harsh, abrasive noise that sounded more like a shovel being thrust into dry, pebbly soil. As I focused on the sound, trying to pin down its source, the scratching blended into something else, something that sounded vaguely like a low, whispered voice.

"Is someone there?" I called out and my words were muffled inside my head as if my ears were filled with water.

There was no reply. I didn't really expect one, but the dull scuffing sound did suddenly stop, leaving behind a dense, throbbing vacuum. Nearly frantic, I looked around the room. I needed to run, but I had no idea which way to go. There were gaping, dark doorways on all four walls. The darkness within all of them fairly vibrated with pitch black shadows.

"Who's there?" I called out again, my voice weak and scared, almost breaking in my throat. "What do you want?"

My eyes shifted again to the two coffins in the center of the room, but complete darkness had surrounded them now and I could no longer make them out.

Just at the edge of hearing, I heard a voice whispering softly.

Come with me. You need to see this.

At that moment I again heard the shovel digging into pebbly earth, and I started walking forward, toward the nearest door. It didn't matter where it led. I had to leave this room. I had to find a way out of this nightmare before it was too late.

The open doorway swelled with darkness so thick it seemed to be a living, breathing thing. As I felt myself being drawn toward the opening, the rough scraping sound rose even louder until it grated on my nerves. I suddenly realized that the sound was coming from the darkness beyond the doorway.

I had a sudden vision of the grim reaper digging my

grave. Pure, blinding panic filled me. I tried to turn away and run, but the doorway continued to draw me forward.

Welcome home, Sam, a papery-thin voice whispered. *We've been waiting for you.*

I'd never forgotten that first day at Farnham House, how I was convinced that someone had spoken those exact words in a moment of strangeness unlike anything else in my experience.

"Somebody, please . . . help me," I called out, and then my voice stretched out into a long, keening wail. The closer I got to the door, the more the darkness within the doorway resolved, taking on a series of undulating shapes.

For a paralyzing instant, I didn't recognize what they were, but then I saw that the darkness had assumed the form of several gauzy but human forms.

Ghosts.

I wanted to scream but couldn't. I could see them, waiting for me in the darkness beyond the doorway, arms outstretched and anxious to take me into their embrace. I could see the smoky undulations of black against black; I could almost feel the iron-tight grip of arms closing around my body, of hands at my throat crushing the life out of me.

Welcome home, Sam. We've been waiting for you.

Using every ounce of effort I could muster, I turned and began to run.

I didn't care where. All I knew was, I had to get away from the door and the shadowy figures that beckoned there. My bare feet whispered on the carpet like high, panting breaths as I dashed across the living-room floor and through one of the other doorways. I had no idea where it led and I didn't care. My only thought was, I had to get away from those terrible shadows. My shoulders and the back of my neck were prickling with knots of icy tension because I knew they were coming for me; somehow I knew they were closing the distance between us. Their hands were hooked like claws, ready to snag me and drag me down. I grabbed the edge of the door jamb and wheeled around as I darted into what turned out to be a long, narrow corridor. It was dimly lit, but light enough for me to see. I stumbled as a terrible groan wrenched from my throat.

All the while, I knew they were directly behind me. I didn't have to turn and look; I could feel their awful presence just inches away, breathing down my neck. And I could feel that their souls were anguished beyond articulation. Then I suddenly knew who they were. They were the souls of those who'd died inside this house. And I knew what they wanted. They wanted me, another soul to further fuel their anguish.

As I ran, the corridor seemed to lengthen, telescoping crazily away from me. Numerous doors lined both sides of it, and I could see that some of them were open.

Through the widening cracks, I caught fleeting glimpses of more people inside the rooms—shadowy figures that reached out for me as I ran past them.

Welcome home, Sam. We've been waiting for you.

I knew that even the slightest faltering of my pace would be disastrous. They would catch me and then . . .

Please don't catch me, I kept thinking as I fought back panic and tried to think clearly. Where can I go? How can I get rid of them? They had all gathered from out of the many rooms now, and were moving swiftly behind me, like winged shadows of the night. No matter how hard I ran, the distant, dark end of the corridor seemed to telescope away from me.

The floor pitched violently, at crazy angles that threw me off balance. My arms flailed wildly, and I tried to scream but couldn't. My breath was burning like acid in my throat and lungs.

Suddenly, with the fluidity of dreams that only makes sense within a dream, I found myself running in another place, and as I ran, I realized that this was no longer the house of my childhood, the house I had grown to the age of twelve in—this was the cellar of Farnham house. I ducked beneath low, cobwebbed rafters and sections of brand new chrome heat pipe as I ran deeper into the bowels of the basement, all the while terribly aware that the shadowy ghosts were still behind me, relentlessly dogging my every step. The cellar turned into a long, twisting tunnel whose distant end was lost in darkness. The rough scraping sound that filled my ears might have been my own breathing—or the sound of my bare feet skidding on the dirt floor—but the more I thought about it, the more I realized that it was a shovel digging a grave—my grave—in dry pebbly soil. My mind was a raging white blank of terror as I forced myself to keep running, even though I knew that I was close to collapse. Somehow—amazingly—I kept going, fleeing from one kind of darkness into another.

Up ahead I spotted the Hulk, with its grinning maw of a mouth. As I moved toward it, I felt no comfort seeing it because beyond the louvers, on the inside of the firebox, the Hulk was burning ferociously, orange and yellow flame dancing and roaring. My heart sank. It was as if I was being herded by dozens of shadowy ghosts into the fiery maw of hell.

I knew in my heart that it couldn't actually *be* the Hulk, because this was a dream. In reality the furnace had not yet undergone its first test firing since being rebuilt. I had just this morning spoken with Carlisle about it and he assured me that the time was close but there was still some tweaking left to do before the test firing could be accomplished. Even so, there was something horribly real about the entire experience of this dream.

Welcome home, Sam, the Hulk seemed to say. *We've been waiting for you.*

You want me to burn. Is that what this is about?"

We want you to see.

We want you to understand.

What do you want me to understand?

Why you came to this place.

Tell me!

You cannot know until you know.

That doesn't even make sense.

Again with an abrupt but perfectly acceptable dreamlike shift, I realized that I was now inside another house running for my life. Not my parent's house, and not the basement of Farnham House. This time I was upstairs in Farnham House. There was no furniture, and the walls were all a dull gray. Obviously it was the Farnham House of yesteryear, long before we ever came here. I saw windows with tattered shades partially raised. As I glanced left and right, I saw ink-dark silhouettes shifting like smoke in all of the windows, and I caught the faint glow of dozens of eyes, sparkling in the dark as they stared at me with cold, bitter malice.

As I ran, all the glittering eyes left their places and chased after me. I could hear the rasping of heavy breathing and the sounds of anguish keeping pace with my every footstep. I could almost smell their sweat and their fear. I wondered if they were keeping their distance to tease me, to toy with me. At any moment, I fully expected them to spring forward, and then I would feel cold, powerful hands grab me and take me down. I needed to understand why these restless spirits wanted me. But I thought I knew. Their spirits were not yet resolved. They needed closure. That's why I had come here, to give them closure.

But why me?

How could I give them closure?

They want me to burn!

The thought filled me with a gnawing dread certainty. No matter where I go, no matter what I do they'll always be here with me. And eventually they're going to get their way.

In another sudden and dizzying dream shift I was outside running along a darkened, storm ravaged road. Swaying trees towered above me, their branches laced together to block out any light from the night sky. My feet slapped the ground, but the gravel hurt my bare feet, making it difficult to keep my balance. Rain sheeted across me, and several times, I stumbled and almost fell; and still, the shadowy figures dogged my every step. But how? Why couldn't they just leave me alone?

Wind was whistling in my ears with a dull, hollow sound that spread chills up and down my back. Pain and exhaustion sizzled like electricity inside me, sapping my strength. There was no hope. No escape. I was doomed. A great sadness welled up inside me, almost overwhelming. Finally, in resignation, I slowed my pace, and then drew to a halt, panting heavily. I wanted to turn and face the shadow people, but all I could do was close my eyes and cringe, waiting for them to swoop down and have their way with me. For a terrifying, timeless moment, I waited, and finally the fear and panic inside me subsided as I accepted my fate.

But nothing happened.

Then, at some indistinct point, just below the rapid thundering of my pulse, I became aware of a faint whining sound.

I opened my eyes and looked into the swelling storm to see the minivan carrying Linda, Sean, and perhaps Carlisle rounding a bend in the road. The whining was the sound of the vehicle's tires as they tracked over the rain-slicked blacktop.

For the entire length of this long and terrible nightmare I'd been trying to shake off the shadow people who had been relentlessly dogging me. Now, like an expulsion of pent-up breath they were gone, deserting me like rats deserting a sinking ship, moving toward the oncoming minivan and spreading out across the highway. I saw it all too clearly, and I was powerless to prevent it. I waved my arms and tried to scream, to warn Linda, but it was too late. Through the windshield I saw her give the wheel a violent twist, sending the minivan careening wildly. I screamed as colored lights exploded around me.

Then the dream changed again and the flashing lights of emergency vehicles were everywhere, surrounding the twisted wreckage of two automobiles. I was struggling to understand. I'd only seen one vehicle; our minivan. I'd seen the shadow people block the road, and then the blinding crash. Where had the other vehicle come from?

I tried to get close to our minivan, but now I no

longer recognized it as our minivan. Suddenly I was very confused. Men wearing uniforms were holding me back, sadly shaking their heads.

"It was the shadow people," I said. "They've been chasing me. When they saw the car they lined up across the road. They caused this to happen."

The uniformed men stared at me with a mixture of confusion and pity.

"Shadow people?" one of the officers repeated.

"Yes, they're from the house. The ones that burnt in the fire. And the boys were there, too. The ones that were murdered. I saw them. They were all there, and there were more. How many have died in that house?"

"Sir, you must be mistaken."

"No! Please, you have to believe me. You have to help them."

"There's nothing we can do for them, Mr. Cabot. They're gone."

"Gone?" I said as I cried out in grief. "No! It can't be. Not my wife and child. They can't be gone. They're the loves of my life."

"No, Mr. Cabot, you're confused. Your parents were the ones killed in that car, not your wife and child."

*

I awoke shaking and sobbing. Linda was standing over me.

"You had a bad dream," she said, gazing into my wet eyes. "And it was a noisy one. Are you okay?"

"I don't know," I said, even as relief washed over me like a warm tide. "I think so."

Linda was still looking at me, her face clouded with

concern. "You sure?"

"Yeah, I think so."

"Sam, you're all sweaty. And there's blood on your feet." Linda took one of my bare feet in her hands and inspected the soul. "Jesus, Sam, they're all scraped and scratched. What the hell have you been doing?"

Panic nearly overwhelmed me in that moment as Linda rushed to the kitchen sink to retrieve a wet washcloth.

"Nothing," I called after her. "I fell asleep."

She came back and sponged off the bottoms of my feet. "They don't look too bad. You've been walking in your sleep again, haven't you?"

"I don't know. Maybe."

"Damn it, Sam, you're scaring the hell out of me."

"I'm okay. Listen, where's Sean?"

"In the kitchen. We're lugging in groceries."

"Let me help."

"No, you stay right where you are until we're done and I'll put some bandages on those cuts."

I nodded. It took me a few long moments to get my panic under control. I realized that Linda was probably right. I'd been sleep walking. There could be no other explanation for my injured feet.

We want you to see.

We want you to understand.

The problem was, I didn't see, nor did I understand. In truth I was more confused now than ever before.

The dream would not go away. It haunted me for months.

Chapter 12

By Labor Day, the Hulk was finally up and running. I was in awe of it, of course, as I knew I would be, marveling at its size and complexity, fawning over it like a car-nut with a newly restored '55 Chevy. Carlisle stood back watching my reaction, assuring me of its efficiency and necessity. He needn't have bothered, I was hooked beyond articulation.

When it was time for the test burn, my face went waxy with a fine sheen of cold sweat and my hands shook like a man with palsy. As fuel entered the burner, misted in the firebox and ignited, the roar sounded as strange and as wonderful to me as the breathing of some newly-awakened beast.

*

Linda enrolled Sean in first grade at Davenport Elementary School. The days continued to stay warm right into September. I promised Sean we'd take him to the beach carnival on the following Saturday. It was going to be our first weekend off in more than three months. But we didn't go to the carnival on that day. A cold rain fell instead. The first blustery feel of fall was in the air. What a strange turn of events. Or perhaps not so strange at all, now that I can look at everything clearly and put it into perspective. Things were starting to come apart in and around our dream house by that time. Change had come to Farnham House. I wasn't exactly sure what, but something felt different. I knew it in my bones. My moods continued to darken as Linda and I drifted further and further apart. And it was somehow all related to two things:

that strange dream I'd had the month before, and the attraction I felt when I came within range of the Hulk, which began to worsen, morphing into something like obsession.

I wandered a lot in those days, awake and asleep, and without realizing it I would find myself in the basement, standing trancelike in front of that huge shiny life-force, staring at the fire behind the louvered maw of a door and wondering what it would feel like to burn.

Chapter 13

The saying goes that omens come in threes. The Hulk, the well, and now the mask. I should have known then—and probably did on some subterranean level—that the mask was somehow connected to it all. It was odd how we came upon the mask in the first place. I suppose it was inevitable. It had been there all along, in that old trunk in the attic waiting for a rainy day so that it could be discovered.

Up until that time we hadn't had a chance to explore the attic. Carlisle had discouraged us on that first day and we'd been just too damned busy during the summer. Sure, I got up there a few times in the process of doing my restorations, but it was never for exploration purposes. It was to run wiring and install roof vents and such. Carlisle had been right. The place was cluttered with old junk and Linda was just itching to pick through it.

But before I get to that, let me tell you about the events leading up to the discovery of the mask.

*

The night before the discovery, I had another wrenching dream. The shadow people were there again, this time in my bedroom, looming above me. They were just featureless silhouettes, as black as holes that had been ripped in the night; only their glittering eyes gave them life.

We want you to see.

We want you to understand.

They were trying to communicate something to me. I know that now. I wish I had known what then.

Welcome home, Sam, We've been waiting for you.

I felt claustrophobic, like I was suffocating. I heard a voice, a shrill, rising scream that took me a few minutes to recognize as my own. I was still screaming when my eyes snapped open. The room was dark. I realized I was sitting up in bed and my fists were swinging, every muscle in my body tensed. I swung out blindly with both fists the instant I sensed someone come up close beside me. I connected with something, but I could tell there wasn't nearly enough power in it to do damage. My feet thrashed wildly, but I couldn't kick free of the tangle of sheets.

"Damn it, Sam! Stop it! For God sakes, it's me!"

The voice was loud enough and close enough to hurt my ears, but through my blinding panic, I didn't recognize it. Terror filled me as I felt someone grab hold of my arms to try and steady me. "Come on, stop it. It's just a dream. You're having another nightmare."

At last Linda's voice registered. I let my body relax and in that instant all strength drained out of me. Sighing, I slumped back onto the bed, my body slick with sweat. When I drew a deep breath my chest hurt as if ribs were broken.

"You're okay. You're okay," Linda said soothingly. I was aware that she was holding onto me tightly.

"Jesus, Sam, this is getting out of hand," she said.

I licked my lips and looked around, but the bedroom was too dark to see very well. Linda was just an indistinct form. For all I knew this might not be Linda at all but one of the shadow people who had assumed her shape and voice to trick me.

"Are you okay now?"

"Shit," I whispered, letting myself fall back on the damp sheets and closing my eyes. As my pulse gradually slowed and my breathing returned to normal I tried to push the nightmare images out of my mind, but the cold, stark terror of the shadow people would not go away.

"Shit," I whispered again.

After another few seconds, I felt Linda move from the bed and go to the window where she drew the curtain aside. I cautiously opened my eyes. The light was dim, nevertheless it hurt my eyes. I was relieved to see that it really was Linda standing there.

"Just like old times, huh?" Linda said.

"I don't know what you mean?"

"Your PTSD, Sam. Don't try to deny it."

I shook my head. No, I wasn't going to deny it, much as I knew these dreams weren't about Afghanistan. They were about something much closer and scarier.

"You used to scare the crap out of me with your PTSD nightmares. Then things were good for a long time. But since we came to this house. . ." Linda let the thought trail off as she hugged her arms to her body.

I looked at her for another few seconds without speaking, then she sighed and shook her head.

"What's going on, Sam?" she asked looking scared.

I knew I should have been honest with her but what would I have said? *This is about something much closer to our lives than a distant war on terror. I keep having this dream where all the people who died in our house—the ones I never told you about—keep trying to warn me about something bad. Oh yeah, and the furnace talks to me all the time too, you know, like it's not a furnace at all but some sort of living creature. I think it wants me to burn and I don't seem to have the courage to resist it. And truth is I can't talk to you about any of this because I've been warned against it. And if none of this is real, well, I'm afraid it would just reinforce my increasing belief—and yours, by the way— that I need a nice little vacation on the padded cell side of the loony bin. Now do you understand?*

In the end I gave her the simplest answer I could and still maintain some semblance of dignity. "Nothing's going on."

Biting her lower lip, Linda shook her head, turned away and left the room.

Chapter 14

When I came downstairs she was standing, her back to me at the stove in her housecoat, cracking eggs into a stainless-steel bowl. Beyond her, through the kitchen window, rain fell in sheets. Sean was zipping around the table holding a balsa-wood airplane above his head making a noise similar to that of a chain-saw on the verge of cuffing a piston rod.

"Grrrrrrrrr, rrrrrr, rrrr," he went as he cruised around the room. "Grrrrrrrrrr, rrrr, rrr, Grrrrrrrrrrr, rrrr, rrr, Grrrrrrrrrr, rrrr, rrr."

"Are you sure you're all right, Cabot?" Linda asked without turning to speak directly to me.

"Yeah, I think so," I said, having to shout in order to get above Sean's racket.

"I heard you get up in the night," she said, "sometime before you had that awful nightmare. It seemed a long time before you came back to bed."

I knew where I'd been, of course. It seemed in recent weeks I would automatically get up in the night and go down into the basement without the benefit of free will. Not exactly sleep-walking, but something similar, I suppose—perhaps it had been something more trance-induced—that left me without much of a memory of the incident when morning came. It didn't matter. The memory part anyway. How I ended up there was secondary. What I was doing there was the important part. But now I was beginning to wonder if Linda knew more than I gave her credit for.

"Grrrrrrrrr, rrr, rr," Sean went, cruising back and forth in front of my face.

"Sean," I said calmly. "Please go into the living room and watch TV until breakfast is ready. You're getting on my nerves."

"Oh, Daddy."

"You heard your father," Linda said. She turned from the stove and Sean stopped dead in his tracks. She was edgy and I could see it on her face and read it in her posture, that harried look one gets when they've reached the end of their proverbial rope.

Sean saw it too. "Sesame Street, Sesame Street," he blurted as he and his airplane flew toward the living room at speeds approaching the sound barrier.

"Now, what were you saying?"

Linda looked at me. "Goddammit!" she said. "He never sits still. He's like a hyperactive little monkey. He's driving me crazy. Sometimes I feel like running away." She held the spatula in her hand and I could see a swell of tears in her eyes. "You need to be firmer with him."

"Don't start in on me again, Linda. I'm doing the best I can."

"Okay, smart ass, have it your way." She aimed the spatula at me, and her eyes drew down, narrow and accusing. "But don't come crying to me when he's beyond our control. Now is when he needs the guiding hand of a father, not ten years from now."

"He's just hyperactive, that's all!"

"Yes, I know. The doctor says he has ADHD. Well you know something? Sometimes I think people like Carlisle are smarter than we give them credit for. I think the medical establishment makes up these disorders because people are gullible and believe them and it makes doctors rich. There. That's what I *really* think. What Sean needs is a father."

"Wait a minute. That's not fair—"

"Isn't it, Sam? Think about it. You hardly ever give

him any special time. You're either working on the house or you're writing in those loose leaf notebooks of yours."

"This house is what we wanted, isn't it? You begged me to buy it."

"I know, I did. And I'm starting to regret it."

"And I'm trying to write a novel."

"But you also have a family."

Linda was right, of course. It wasn't the first time in recent weeks that we'd had this discussion. I knew that my responsibility as a father and a husband was somehow slipping away from me. I knew that I was on some sort of descent, and powerless in the face of it. Linda knew it too, but she was just as powerless as I was.

"All right," I said, and I could feel my face flushing with anger. "From now on I'll make sure and beat him once a day whether he needs it or not."

And the moment the words were out of my mouth I knew that it had been the wrong thing to say. Linda stood with her back to me, rigid, seething. Then she turned, stood with hands on hips, and said, "What's going on, Cabot?"

"I don't know."

"Don't lie to me! You think I imagine you getting out of our bed every night and not coming back for hours? I want to know what's going on. What's wrong with you? What's wrong with *me?*"

My eyes dropped to the floor. "I don't know." I said, in a small, defeated voice, and it was the truth, sort of. What else could I say? I was not allowed to talk about the Hulk or what I had been learning from it. This was clear. It would have killed my family if I had. And besides, I didn't actually *know* what I was learning.

Not yet anyway. It was sort of like the first stages of some weird foreign language. Clarity would come eventually, I was sure of that. The part I wasn't sure about was whether I would like the lesson once it had finally been grasped.

"And when you *are* in bed," Linda went on, "you have nightmares. You talk in your sleep. You walk in your sleep. I try to wake you, but you won't wake up. This morning you almost punched me out, for cripes sake."

"Tell me something, Linda, what do I talk about in these nightmares?"

"Do you really want to know?"

"Yes I really do."

"Okay, here goes, but if you try to punch me out again I'm leaving you, Cabot."

"Linda, tell me."

Linda stared at me for a long moment before answering. Finally she said, "Okay, shadow people. What the hell are shadow people? And the Hulk. You mean like the comic strip guy they made a TV show about? Why are you dreaming about a comic strip character? A lot of it is gibberish. Ghosts chasing you and lining up across the road. What's that supposed to mean? You sound like a mad man. You used to have some pretty creepy nightmares after you got back from Afghanistan. Back then you needed a shrink. I understand. War sucks and it screws people up. Nothing to be ashamed of. If you want the truth, I think the bad stuff has started up again and it's scaring the crap out of me. I think you need to go back to the VA and make an appointment with a shrink. I think you've got some serious issues, and lord knows, you never come to me for help. I don't know, maybe you're beyond my help."

I knew what the nightmares were about, of course, and Afghanistan wasn't it; it was the dream of the accident, the day Linda and Sean had given Carlisle a ride to town. Somehow I kept coming back to that in my thoughts and in my nightmares. In the dream I was confused about whether it was my parents who'd died or whether it had been Linda and Sean. But of course it wasn't Linda and Sean. They were here, alive and well. My parents were long gone and their deaths had dropped me into a chasm of despair that had taken me all the way into adulthood to climb out of.

"There's nothing you can do for them, Mr. Cabot. They're gone."

"Sam, are you listening to me?"

I started. Linda had been talking and again I was reliving that horrible time. Why was it haunting me so? Would I ever be able to put it behind me?

Linda walked over to the table with a steaming pan of scrambled eggs. Oscar the Grouch grumbled in the living room. She leaned in toward me and said in a whisper, "Sam, I'm scared. There's something wrong here. I feel it and I think Sean feels it too. Sean," she called. "Come eat your breakfast."

"I think you're worrying for nothing," I said. "This is all so new to us. The house, this life. We've been working our asses off. We haven't had time for anything else but this house. But we're almost done. Things will get better, I promise."

"I don't feel like things are getting better."

"You just need to buck up, that's all."

"Don't you dare make light of this, Sam. I'm starting to freak out. I'm worried about you. I'm worried about *us.*"

"Please don't," I said in a consoling voice. "I'm okay, honest." I gave her a small and playful pat on the bottom.

"No, you're not!" she said, pulling away from me almost violently. "You're freaking me out."

"And you're taking drugs," I shot back. "I saw the Valium on your bedside stand."

"I'm taking valium because I'm scared," Linda said. "I'm taking it so that I can get a decent night's sleep. I'm afraid of what's inside *you*, Sam. Don't you get it? I'm scared."

"You're afraid of me?"

"Yes!"

The TV clicked off, and for a fleeting moment the whole world was utterly silent. Then the house groaned loudly, as old houses sometimes do. Sean flew into the kitchen, his eyes bulging with fright. Linda and I looked at each other and burst out laughing.

"What was that, Daddy?"

"Just the house settling," I said. "These old houses do it all the time."

The terror in Sean's eyes would not go away, however. "The TV spoke to me," he said.

"What?" Linda's face crumpled.

I said, "Don't be ridiculous, Sean."

"I'm not."

"Well, what did it say?"

'Mustn't tell what's in the well. Mustn't tell what's in the well. Mustn't tell what's in the well.' It kept saying it over and over again and then it shut off all by itself. I saw smoke."

All the color blanched from my face. I felt it happen. Linda stood rigid, unable to react.

"You must have misunderstood, son. The only

thing I heard was old Oscar the Grouch blabbing away. You must have thought he was talking to you."

"No, Daddy, it did say it, honest. *'Mustn't tell what's in the well. Mustn't tell what's in the well. Mustn't tell what's in the well.* Sean began hyper-cruising again, sounding like a stuck record.

"Sit down and eat your breakfast, now!" I told him, losing my patience. Sean plunked himself down at his place at the table and burst into tears.

"Jesus!" Linda said and went to comfort him.

I walked into the living room and sure enough, smoke was belching from the back of the television set. I grabbed hold of the heated electrical cord and pulled. Sparks flew as the plug popped from the wall socket. At least the smoking began to subside. And then, just as plain as day, I heard Carlisle's voice say, *"Don't forget our little secret, Sam. Mustn't tell what's in the well."* For a moment, I could not breathe. Panic gripped me like sickness and I thought I would scream. Instead I said, "You leave my son out of this, you old bastard."

"Too late, Sam. You know he's in it all the way."

I walked trance-like back into the kitchen and there behind Linda stood a group of undulating human-shaped figures so black they could have been cookie-cut from the darkness of the night. All had glittering eyes filled with so much menace I actually feared for Linda's safety. "Look out!" I screamed and the shadow people vanished into vapor.

Sean suddenly stopped bawling. He put his hand over his mouth and giggled.

Linda said, "See what I mean, Cabot. This place is creepy. And *you're* getting creepier by the minute. What am I going to do with you?" She glared narrowly at me.

I blinked and stared dumbly, unable to speak,

suddenly unsure of anything at all.

*

After the breakfast dishes had been cleaned up was when we decided to explore the attic for the first time. The mask had been packed away in an old trunk that was tucked up under the eaves, along with a bunch of other useless junk. When Linda pulled it out and put it to her face, such a feeling of horror and dismay rose in me that for one small moment I thought I might go mad. You see, I recognized it; it was the face I'd seen in the well, my own reflection mutating into something horrific.

For a long time I just stood there hearing the rain lashing against the house with each gust of wind, the attic moaning as the wind whistled through the rafters.

Mustn't tell what's in the well.

I sensed some kind of twisted truth in that mask, although at the time I could not fathom just what that truth was.

It was a fluorescent-green thing, an unidentifiable creature somewhere between human and beast with large grinning teeth and eyes the color of urine, so grotesque it was almost comical. The mask appeared quite old, probably p*apier-mâché*, some left over whimsy from a long forgotten masquerade party, or a theater costume mask from some bygone stage production. How on earth it got into that old trunk in the attic of our house I'll probably never know.

"That's neat," said Sean, reaching up toward his mother's face for the mask. "Can I have it?"

"I don't see any reason why not," Linda said.

"No!" I screamed. *Calm yourself, Cabot. It's only a*

mask. There's no reason to go getting your family all upset over this. But I wasn't feeling the way I was thinking. It took an incredible amount of effort to get myself under control. Linda was looking at me as if I'd lost my mind. And I might have. "Put it back in the trunk," I said as calmly as I could, not knowing whether it had been good enough to fool Linda. The mask grinned at me from Linda's hand. I felt hot and flushed and my mouth was dry and coppery tasting. "God knows how many rats have made nests in there," I said, speaking of the trunk. In reality I would have said anything to make her put that mask back in the trunk. My fear of it was off the charts. I did not want it near my wife and child. I wanted it back in the trunk, and I wanted it there as quickly as possible.

"Rats?" Linda said.

"Yeah, rats," I repeated, continuing on with the lie. "Rats live in those kinds of places. And they carry disease.

"Stop it, Sam."

"I'm not kidding."

"Oh dear," she said looking disdainfully at the mask in her hand.

Outside a gust of wind rocked the house, causing the old timbers in the attic to creak and cackle eerily.

Sean stepped closer to me and clung to my leg. "What was that, Daddy?" he asked as the gust died to a low, steady hum.

"Just the wind," I managed through lips that felt like they'd been shot full of Novocain. I was still looking at the mask in Linda's hand; its green-veined forehead, its sickly yellow eyes, its idiot grin. "Wind plays funny tricks around the eaves of old houses," I said. "Sometimes it sounds like voices. Like old ladies cackling."

Sean giggled a little nervously. "Yeah, old ladies cackling," he repeated.

Linda dropped the mask back into the trunk, brushed her hands together with something like revulsion, and moved away to examine an old box filled with dusty knickknacks. Apparently, my explanation had been good enough to get her to relinquish the mask to its hiding place. Obviously, she hadn't been alarmed by my panic, or if she had been she didn't let on.

I ducked under the slant of the roof where rusty nails protruded. I quickly dropped the lid of the trunk and turned the latch, feeling better almost immediately, but still uneasy. I caught myself wishing for a key so that I might lock the mask away forever.

The wind was louder now, roaring through the roof-vents. The attic creaked, waxing and waning, making noises similar to those of a wooden ship in heavy seas. Outside, rain pelted down.

Sean's blue eyes looked afraid. "I wanta go downstairs, Daddy."

"Okay, champ. Linda, let's go!"

"I'd like to look around a bit more." she said a little testily. "*If* you don't mind."

"Be my guest," I said. "Sean and I are heading down."

Linda's eyes drew down on me. "Another time?" she said. I nodded.

Chapter 15

Time passed strangely from then on. I don't think I really forgot about the mask, although it never consciously entered my mind again. It was in there, though, neatly tucked away in my psyche, like dust bunnies beneath parlor furniture.

I began to write again. Linda and I chose one of the more spacious downstairs rooms—a room which had once been the parlor—and converted it into a study. It was perfect. An old bay window gave way to a view of the expansive back yard and the trees beyond. I set my desk and word processor up so as to take full advantage of the panoramic view.

The novel proceeded nicely. I had never felt so prolific. Linda continued to fine-tune our environment with antiques and used furniture acquired at local fairs and flea markets which she would painstakingly strip and refinish. She decorated rooms with bright bouquets of late summer shrubs and flowers. Despite all our problems we both made an effort to keep things together, going about our daily lives as if nothing was wrong.

Painting contractors replaced broken clapboards and primed the exterior of the house in preparation for the inevitable winds of winter, and when they had finally picked up and left, we were alone for the first time since acquiring the place, save Carlisle's regular but diminishing appearances and the occasional visit from John and Meg.

Indian summer came that year in all of her usual and glorious splendor, and then she left us suddenly. Too suddenly, like a broken promise, her scarlets and ochers turning to rust, drifting languidly on the heels of a chilled October wind.

From my study window I watched Carlisle—oftentimes with Sean at his side—rake leaves into huge piles and set them ablaze, sending gray smoke wafting up into an even grayer sky, a sky that held the promise of winter.

*

One mid-morning near the end of the month, a man appeared at our door. Actually he was no more than a kid, tall and thin with a thick head of wavy brown hair; his dark eyes were intelligent and inquiring behind thick horned-rimmed glasses. "I'm with the State Health Department," he said, offering his hand. "Linwood Devlin's the name, clean water's my game." He smiled at his own lame joke and said, "You Mr. Cabot?"

"Yes," I said, standing there on the stoop wondering what a man from the health department could want with me. And then suddenly it struck me. "Clean water," I said. "Now I get it. You're here about the well out back, aren't you?"

"That's right," Devlin said. "We'd like a clean sample. There seems to be a lot of strange organic stuff in it."

"I expected you in the summer," I replied. "I'd almost forgotten about it."

"Been busy," he explained. "You know how these bureaucracies work."

I nodded. "What's so strange about there being organic material in the well?" I asked. "This is Planet Earth. There's organic matter everywhere."

"Not like this," he said. "Listen, I'm not supposed

to alarm you."

"Alarm me?" I said, now quite alarmed. "This is my home. I have a right to know what's down there."

The young man was silent for a long moment, staring at me. It was impossible to read his expression. His Adams apple bobbed a couple of times with a forced swallow, and then he said, "Listen, sir, we're really not sure. That's why I'm here. It's possible that when you took that first sample you contaminated it somehow."

"Contaminated it? With what?"

"The jar you used might not have been sterilized."

"It was clean," I said, but he was right, I hadn't bothered to *sterilize* it. Just the same, I wondered what sort of strange organic matter could survive inside of a clean Mason jar. I remembered the smell of the stuff that came out of that well and knew it wasn't something inside the jar.

"Listen, Mr. Cabot. It would be useless for me to try and explain what's in that well when we don't even know yet. It would be better if you'd just let me take the samples. I'm sure the State will let you know as soon as they have something conclusive."

I nodded. "Come in." Linda and Meg were shopping in town; no telling how long they'd be, and Sean was in school. I'd been in my study since seven that morning writing, but to tell you the truth, I was glad for the diversion. I went in and turned off my computer and asked the young man if he'd like something to drink.

"No, thanks," he replied, looking at his watch. "I'm on a pressed schedule and really must get down to business. Lot of bad wells this year."

I put on a jacket and took Devlin out back to show

him the well. I stood back away from the thing, still having a bad taste in my mouth about what had happened earlier in the summer.

He carried a small black suitcase with him, laid it on the ground and proceeded to open it. He extracted a coiled length of thin yellow nylon rope and a small sealed stainless-steel vial with a baled handle. He tied the rope to the handle and set the container on the brown grass. Next he extracted a hammer, two small lidded boxes and two pointed metal tubes about a foot long each. He drove the tubes into the earth at ten and twenty foot intervals from the well, extracted them carefully from the ground and deposited the soil samples into the boxes. Then he took a grease pencil and marked the samples. Afterward, he went over to the well, lifted one side of the oak platform and slid the cover aside. I watched him carefully peer down and I involuntarily flinched. But the young man stepped back, expressionless. I felt a wave of relief. Obviously he hadn't seen anything unusual. He gathered up the coiled length of rope and the vial, unscrewed the cover and broke the hermetic seal. Next, he lowered the vial slowly into the depths. I heard the small splash of water at the bottom and then he began to pull it back. The rope suddenly fetched up on something.

"Careful," I said, feeling my heartbeat quicken.

He tugged lightly on the rope and grunted in agitation, bending over the edge, trying to get a better look at what had caused the snag. I remembered the slight tug I'd felt on my rope when I'd tried to reel it in earlier that summer and the quick moment of panic I'd felt. This kid wasn't feeling any panic, though, I could tell. He was used to this sort of thing. He'd probably done it in a thousand different wells and had been snagged up half of those times.

"What's the problem?" I asked trying to sound calm, but I wasn't calm. My heart rate had picked up and now I could feel sweat beads breaking out on my brow despite the cool October air.

"Snagged," he replied. "Don't want to lose the container. He leaned further out over the rim and hitched the line toward the other side like a trout fisherman gingerly trying to release his line from the bottom without scaring the fish. I was just about to warn him to be careful when there was a sudden and violent downward-tug on the line. Devlin nearly lost his balance. He turned to me as if to say, *what the fuck,* but the words that might have been, never got spoken.

"Jesus, watch out!" I said stepping forward, but the warning came too late. In the midst of it, the line pulled taut once again, this time with violence that astonished me, but instead of letting go of the rope as he should have, it seemed the young man's grip actually tightened on it. Devlin was yanked forward off balance. The rope sang through his hands at flesh-singeing speed. He screamed in pain and finally let go of the rope altogether, too late, however, for that second and most violent tug had caused him to lose his balance completely. His arms began rotating furiously forward as he tried to regain his balance. I was in motion and tried to reach him, but I wasn't fast enough. Devlin took a step forward; it was the only way he could regain his balance, and in so doing, one leg walked off into space. The upper part of his body keeled forward and his head struck the rim of the well with a sound like a ripe melon striking pavement. The sharp blow pitched him violently backwards where he tumbled completely upside-down and sailed headfirst into the depths, disappearing from view in an instant. I heard a long, low grunt that was, I suppose, an injured, terrified version of a scream. Then there was a sudden, muffled thud and a small splash of water. Then, silence. I somehow managed the last few steps to the rim and stood there in total shock, looking down, not having the wits to even form a coherent thought. When my brain did finally kick in, my thoughts were all jumbled and full of panic. My stomach heaved and my gorge rose. I swallowed it back, dropping down onto my hands and knees and peering into the depths. I could not find my breath. Tears obstructed my vision as they began to flow. I wiped them away with the sleeve of my shirt.

"Devlin?" I called. "Are you okay?"

Of course he's not okay, this admonishing little voice told me. *He just fell head first into a fucking twenty-five foot deep well.*

I saw nothing at first, just blackness, like a hole drilled into hell. Then I saw the young man's legs sticking up out of that murky pool, splayed, impossibly still. *He's dead,* I thought. *Jesus Christ, he's as dead as a fucking carp. Oh, God please, don't let it be.* Something suddenly moved down there, like a trout rising to a fly, and a small flower of hope blossomed inside of me. "Are you all right?" I yelled again and my voice sounded muffled and distant and a little insane in my own ears. But then I could clearly see that it was not the young man doing the moving. Something else was writhing in those depths. Not a trout. No way. It was something big—something terrible, something I did not want to see but was powerless to pull my eyes away from—circling the submerged part of the young man's torso like a shark circling prey. Then, in a sudden and fierce lunge, it attacked. Water and muck boiled from the well in a violent cascade that nearly reached me as I kneeled, staring fixedly down in horror.

There were no trout in that well. No indeed. There were no sharks in that well. Those kinds of life forms could not exist in such a terrible and toxic place. But there was most assuredly *something* alive in that well, something that relished the taste of human flesh. In those short few seconds I saw it, in all its gruesomeness. It was long and thick, and black beyond comprehension, slimy and sinuous, like a boa constrictor with Satan's face. It was the *mask*, that implacable, yet sinister face with teeth like the louvered bands of the Hulk.

"Oh, Jesus, no" I cried in revulsion, crawling back away from that horrible sight, and the terrible eating noises it was making. I don't actually remember my legs coming between me and the ground, but somehow they were there, shambling my quaking body back across the field toward the sanctity of the house and what was left of my sanity.

Chapter 16

Linda arrived home to a yard full of emergency vehicles. I sat in the kitchen in shock. The cops had been questioning me for nearly two hours. Linwood Devlin's body had been lifted out of the well nearly an hour before. His upper torso was nearly unrecognizable. His face was missing. The skull had cracked open like an egg and Devlin's brain had leaked out. I was told that they were still fishing for it in those murky depths (but learned later that they'd given up without finding it). The police wanted to believe that Devlin's violent plunge into the well had caused the disfiguration. So did I, but I knew better. I had been witness to something extraordinary, something supernatural, something . . . I don't know, maybe something evil beyond articulation. I wasn't about to tell the cops that, though. Even if I'd wanted to—which I didn't—I couldn't have. It would never have been allowed. Something not even close to a conscious thought process, something on a level that was probably ten stories beneath visceral warned me to stay away from such notions.

Mustn't tell what's in the well.

The policemen who handled the body had gagged at the foul jelly-like substance that covered it. I explained the reason for Devlin's visit, that there was an unidentifiable toxin in the well and that he was here for a sample.

"But how did he *fall?*" the policeman, a Lieutenant Atkins kept asking me.

Each time I gave him the same answer, which was: "I don't know."

"But you say you were standing right behind him?"

"Yes," I said for the umpteenth time. "He must have slipped or something. I just don't know. One minute he was there and the next he was gone."

Atkins nodded, but I could see that he wanted more from me.

"Are you insinuating that my husband might have done something to cause his fall?" Linda said outraged.

"No, of course not, Mrs. Cabot," the lieutenant replied. "But we do need to get to the bottom of this." He looked back at me. "Mr. Devlin had rope burns on his hands. Can you explain how they got there?"

"No," I said again. "Maybe it didn't happen here. Maybe it happened on his last job." My voice sounded insanely calm, insanely reasonable.

"We don't think so."

"And what am I to assume by this?"

"By what?" asked the lieutenant, as if he didn't know.

"This interrogation," I said, nearly losing my temper. "Am I under arrest?"

"No, of course not, Mr. Cabot," the lieutenant said, a small acerbic smile on his smug puss. "I can see no reason for that. There doesn't seem to be a motive."

They fished in that murky well for the remainder of the afternoon and all they brought up were buckets-full of toxic sludge that looked and smelled like shit from the bowels of something unholy. They took several samples for testing. After what happened, after all was said and done, they should have been back there like gangbusters filling that hole into hell with whatever they could lay their hands on. But I never heard from them again. I wasn't surprised. I'd seen the looks on their faces when they'd brought Devlin up, and I'd heard the men gag when they'd taken the samples.

No one ever went down there, either, as far as I know, but before leaving they recapped the hole and warned us to stay away from it. As if we had to be told. It's even possible Devlin's death was listed as an accident. I couldn't say for sure. Shortly thereafter I received a letter from the state informing me that someone else would be coming out to do more tests. I wasn't holding my breath. They weren't coming back. That thing I mentioned I had that was about ten floors beneath visceral, well, I think it got those guys, too. Not in quite the same way as me, but it got them, and told them to stay the fuck away. Whatever lived within the periphery of Farnham House and its devil's half-acre could twist your mind into whatever it wanted from you. I wasn't allowed to talk and I don't think they were allowed to remember. But *I* remembered. I found myself thinking about that well a lot after that, and one night I dreamed that there was an underground passage connecting it with the basement and that some unspeakable thing, something slimy and black and hungry, something with the implacable, almost comical face of the mask slunk there in the dark between a sane world where logic reigned and some other world that had most probably tipped dangerously off its axis.

Chapter 17

But, even in a disjointed world, things have a way of normalizing. At least that's the way it felt. To me anyway. I remembered several years earlier living and working in a combat zone, the fear, the apprehension, the uncertainty, and how after a time even that had somehow seemed normal. So I guess it's a matter of perspective.

Sean began bringing home pictures he'd drawn of black cats, jack-o-lanterns, and witches flying on broomsticks in front of gigantic bone-white moons, cold and inhospitable moons that were somehow prophetic in their unyielding and callous equanimity. I shuddered when I looked upon them; my son had innocently drawn them, of course, but I sensed some sort of twisted truth in their alien light, some sort of affirmation that their creator, my son, had tipped slightly off his axis as well.

On Halloween eve, I drove a three-foot ghost through the neighborhood, stopping at houses that belonged to neighbors I had yet the opportunity to meet.

One particular neighbor seemed very afraid when I explained who we were, reinforcing my belief that something in my life, hell, something in *our* lives was tipping dangerously off balance. The woman, a Mrs. Miller, put her hand to her mouth as if to stifle a cry and her body winced. She was frightened. This much was clear. Her bugged-out eyes never left mine as she absently dropped several large handfuls of candy into Sean's trick-or-treat bag.

"So, you're the folks livin up there at the old Carlisle place," she said, her stare icy. "I'll be damned."

"Yes," I said, "but it's no longer the Carlisle place."

"Scuse me?" she said.

"Well, the place is ours now."

Mrs. Miller gave a short, dry little laugh that might have been an asthmatic's version of a cough. "Right," she said. "Let me tell you somethin, mister. It'll always be the Carlisle place."

"I don't know what you mean."

"Well, I'll tell you then. Back in the day, long before the Carlisles owned it, when it was still Farnham House, there was a Carlisle in residence."

"A Carlisle in residence?" I said confused. "How do you mean?"

"If you look back in the records—and believe me, I've done it—all the way back to the early eighteenth century, you'll see that the original innkeeper, a man by the name of William Farnham, brought his own builder and handyman with him from England. And you know what his name was?"

Before I could get a chance to speak Mrs. Miller answered her own question. "His name was Francis Carlisle!" she said. What do you think of that, Mr. Cabot?"

"I don't understand," I said, and it was true. Was it possible that Carlisle's ancestors had stayed on and eventually bought the property from the Farnham estate? Had the original Francis Carlisle had a son who'd had a son and so forth down the line? I stopped as another terrible yet tantalizing possibility began playing around at the fringes of my psyche, a possibility that my sane and rational mind would not allow me to seriously entertain. I could see by the look on Mrs. Miller's face that she knew what I was thinking.

"That's right, Mr. Cabot.

I backed up a step, stunned, totally unable to make sense of any of this.

"The place is tainted by the devil himself," she said. "And his name is Francis Carlisle. Everyone who comes in contact with that place gets tainted. So I'll thank you to stay away from my house from this day forward," she added.

"What did you say?" I asked, suddenly and totally taken aback. The thought crossed my mind that I had encountered a mad woman.

"You and that boy." She pointed at Sean and her eyes narrowed down into hateful little slits. "You've both got it, especially him. I can feel it livin in him like some awful sickness. Like somethin dead that's not really dead. Like death that refuses to die."

"What in God's name are you talking about?" I said, taking Sean by the shoulder and drawing him back away from that hateful woman.

"God's got nothing to do with it," replied the witch. "Maybe the devil, but not God. It comes from Carlisle. He's a cursed soul who wants only blood and sacrifice. It's what got my mother! The same thing everyone who spends time in or around that place gets! *Somethin worse than death!* Someone should've burned that evil place to the ground years ago."

"I don't understand any of this," I said.

"Of course you don't," she replied. "The ones that come under its spell never do."

"Who is your mother?" I asked, but thought I knew.

"Her name was Hattie Dowd. She was Carlisle's old man's housekeeper haunting she died at the insane asylum up at Augusta. She died babbling like a mad woman about what she'd seen and felt in that house and about what got inside her. And you've got it too, I can feel it in you, so please, go away and don't you ever come back here again." With that, Mrs. Miller stepped back and promptly slammed the door in our faces.

*

I was shaken, totally and unequivocally.

So my reaction to what happened when we returned home and I opened the door should not have shaken me further. Yet it did.

I wondered why the house was dark. Not even the porch light burned. In the car's headlights, Farnham House looked like a lonely and abandoned tombstone rising up out of some long-forgotten hilltop graveyard. A sudden and overwhelming fear crawled into my bones. Linda was in there alone.

Oh, God. Where are all the lights? Has something happened to her?

I got out of the car, hurried around to the passenger side and got Sean out. I cradled his small hand in mine and pulled him toward the house's front door, fighting back panic. I turned the knob and pushed the door open. Just beyond the threshold a disembodied face, fluorescent green and horribly grotesque came at me and Sean from out of the gloom.

"Get away!" I screamed stumbling back across the threshold, reaching for my son. I missed him and went down. Sean stood transfixed as the green, disembodied face danced toward him with menacing glee. "Get away!" I screamed again, struggling to my feet, hoping to reach him in time. I thought my pounding heart would burst through my chest. In that split second I saw the mask that had been waiting, biding its time in that old attic trunk, I saw the Hulk's grinning, fiery maw, I saw the face in the well, the death of my parents in an automobile accident in 1988, the horror I had endured in the Afghanistan war. And I saw a reflection of the terrible thing I was becoming, or perhaps the thing I had always been but had never accepted in my true heart. I believed that in that heart-seizing moment of sheer and utter terror, my life, my true life, was in focus as it never had been before. Nothing was sane. Nothing was safe. Madness was beneath everything.

In a blinding flash, the porch light suddenly illuminated, and there stood Linda wearing the mask from the attic. It did not help to know that. My seizing heart went right on seizing. Only now rage had become a part of the mix. I felt like the mask had burned my brain, scorched my soul in some hellish and incomprehensible way. In short, I had become one with the cursed thing. Unwittingly, Linda had allowed me an ominous yet still unreasoned glimpse of a past marred by some indefinable tragedy, a future filled with grief and madness. I stumbled across the threshold toward my wife and angrily ripped the mask from her face, making her wince and draw back in fear.

"Why did you do this?" I screamed, now totally beyond reason.

Linda shrank back against the wall, her mouth slack, her eyes large and round and filled with fear. "It was just a joke," she said. "It's Halloween. Why are you acting this way?"

I dropped the mask abruptly, uttering an unwitting cry of revulsion. It felt as though the loathsome thing had burned my fingers. The touch of it made my skin crawl, and even as it did so, although I was not prepared to admit it just then, I felt it bonding somehow with my flesh, my soul, my being, letting me know that it was all right to slip a little deeper into its hellish spell.

My rage diminishing in nauseous waves, I told Linda never to pull a stunt like that again. She gawked at me with eyes that were oversized wet jewels, bright with terror, wondering, I'm sure, what horrible stunt she *had* pulled. She slid along the wall acting as if I might strike her at any moment. And I might have. She scooped a now weeping Sean up into her arms and ran with him for the stairs, sobbing and cursing God for leading us to this terrible place and time in our lives. And I cursed myself for being what I was becoming, for being what I *was*, even as a part of me rejoiced at the enthralling metamorphosis. I rushed into the bathroom, slid down onto my knees in front of the white porcelain bowl and heaved until I thought the lining of my stomach would come loose. Then I traced my oh-so-familiar route, walking trance-like into the kitchen, down the cellar stairs where I spent the next three hours stroking that loathsome fire-breathing monster, absorbing its sick, prickly heat as it whispered instructions to me in its alien language.

Chapter 18

Linda did not sleep. She wept off and on all through that long night. I lay half in and half out of delirium, hearing whispers in my ears and seeing the mask in my mind, its piss-colored eyes, its gleeful yet merciless grin, feeling its hot, prickly, hellish texture, knowing that it lay on the floor in the living room downstairs inviting me to come and wear it, to *become* it. I did not give in to its dreadful invitation, at least not on that night. Instead I lay in silent torment, torn between light and darkness, sanity and madness, flesh and its myriad corruptions.

The next morning, I arose early and while the house slept, I stole downstairs fully intending to burn the cursed thing in the kitchen woodstove. I walked gingerly around it even as its blank eyes stared implacably up at me. I kindled a fire and made coffee, patiently waiting for the flames to become hot enough to do the job. Then I took the stove poker and carefully picked the mask up off the floor, afraid to touch it with my flesh. I stood transfixed as the thing stared back at me from the end of the poker. Its gaping mouth, studded with large, almost comical-looking teeth, its blank, yellow eyes burning cigarette-holes into my soul. I was unable to draw my gaze from it. It mocked me, I swear it did. *You cannot destroy the force of my determination,* it said, *for that force now lives within you.* In the end it won; I could not destroy the cursed thing. Instead, I took it to the basement and hid it behind an old work bench against the far wall, out of sight, but from then on, never very far from my thoughts.

*

Linda's and my relationship deteriorated to the point of collapse after that. The mask would not go away. If anything, it grew larger inside of me, and it continued to haunt my dreams. In my true heart I understood that it was only a mask, a harmless collage of paper and glue. There was a part of me, however—the part that was about ten levels beneath visceral—that knew it was a symbol for something far greater, something that I could not fathom or reason. In those dreams I began to draw a correlation between the mask, the killer-well in the back yard, and the fiery engine in our basement that now, as winter drew near, seemed to run almost all the time, filling our house with a sick and prickly kind of heat that felt very much like fever. And as this correlation began to crystallize I became more and more determined that there was a secret here, a riddle of some kind that needed to be unraveled, even as my very sanity was unraveling.

I should have taken my family and left that place the day I set eyes on it, but even then it was too late, I was just too blind to know it, and now, the part of me that needed to unravel the mystery was far more persuasive. I had become a prisoner of Farnham House and its terrible secret, and in so doing I had unwittingly doomed my family.

*

Linda did her best to steer clear of me. Thinking back on it now, I realize what a horrifyingly lonely time it must have been for her. We were like strangers in some strange and twisted time-wrinkle that neither of us had the courage or the sense to escape. In a way, Linda went through her own kind of metamorphosis.

She was stronger than I ever gave her credit for, assuming the posture of cool matriarch of the new and increasingly ugly Cabot household, tiptoeing around on eggshells so as not to disturb this strange, ugly Frankenstein monster who sat day and night hunched over his laptop computer. I did not sleep much in those days. When I wasn't writing dark passages I was in the basement stroking that vile metal monster while it repeated its instructions to me over and over again in its alien language.

It went on like this, a seeming endless silence, the only thing breaking the monotony, the sound of the Hulk muttering in the basement as it radiated an oily, repugnant heat that permeated our souls like the plague and did little to take the chill out of the November winds that now howled mournfully around the eaves of Farnham House.

Chapter 19

Sometime toward the middle of November, I awoke one night haunted by a new dream. The bedsheets were soaked where I had lain tossing feverishly, my face was covered with a pillow and my body was shaking with sobs. My tongue was injured and my mouth tasted of blood. I must have cried out because Linda stirred.

"What's wrong?"

"Nothing," I said, trying to sound normal. "Everything's okay. Go back to sleep."

Linda rolled over and did as she was told.

I got up, wringing wet in my bedclothes, went into the bathroom and rinsed my injured mouth with saltwater. The mirror showed an emaciated, nearly unrecognizable man with hollowed cheeks and sunken, dark-rimmed eyes. I was unable to stop trembling as that terrible reflection stared back at me. In a rare moment of clarity, of perhaps even sanity, I wondered what I had become in the months since coming to this house. Had my family succumbed as well? Would I be able to recognize it if it was so?

I went downstairs to my favorite living room chair and sat in the dark waiting for the panic to subside while reflecting on the dream. The grim reaper had been there, hooded and malevolent, shoveling earth into an open grave. The sound his shovel made in the dry, pebbly soil reminded me of the dream I'd had months before where I'd been frantically trying to escape shadow people with glittering eyes while I visited with my long dead parents. In that dream I'd been haunted by the sound of a shovel scraping against dry, pebbly soil. I hadn't been able to articulate that sound until now.

The dream shifted suddenly, as dreams have a way of doing, and I was looking down into the old water-well in the back yard, the one that had swallowed and partially eaten an almost-certainly forgotten young man named Devlin. In the well, Linda and Sean lay on their backs side by side, vacant eyes staring up into a star-studded night sky while earth rained down upon them, clogging their mouths and noses and filling their blank eye sockets. Through some sort of dream magic the well appeared wide enough to hold both prone bodies. I was, it seemed, at least through the initial part of the dream, merely a mute and impartial witness to the horror that was unfolding before me, unable to do or say anything to prevent any of it from happening.

Then the dream changed again and I could see that the reaper was no longer shoveling soil, now he was scooping coal into the Hulk's fiery maw where beyond, Linda and Sean lay placid on a bed of glowing coals. It was to be their crematorium; I understood this on that subterranean plateau I've already discussed at length in this story, that pure and basic animal sense that has nothing whatsoever to do with intellect. I stood and watched as flames licked around them, melting their flesh like wax.

"Used to be a coal furnace," the reaper said, throwing a shovel-full of the dusty black stuff into the Hulk's maw. These were the exact words Carlisle had uttered on our first day at Farnham House, and not surprisingly the reaper sounded very much like Carlisle. But he did not look like Carlisle. As he shoveled, his cowl began to recede and I could see part of the creature that occupied it. It was the mask, of course, its blank, idiot eyes, its eternally implacable grin, its wrinkle-studded skull. The sum of its parts, although nearly comical, were somehow alive and piss-down-your-leg terrifying. It was laughing at me in my terror, in my total inability to react. I tried to speak, but my mouth only made futile sucking sounds like a beached fish desperate for oxygen. And as the cowl slipped further, I began to see that the face was no longer a mask; it had become a living nightmare with expression and nuance, and suddenly it seemed to float there in space, independent of its surroundings, starkly illuminated by the Hulk's terrible death-light. The lips were very still, but as I stared at them they seemed to smile without making the slightest movement.

I tried to move; I needed to get away from that terrible disembodied face, but knew that it would not be allowed. Instead I was drawn to it as an insect is drawn to the sudden electrocution of light. I found myself with my hand outstretched, trying to touch that loathsome face. The thing made no attempt to brush my hand away; instead it floated closer in encouragement even as my entire hand up to the wrist vanished into that awful visage. The feeling was both warm and icy, a prickly feeling, like frostbite. Then a singing arose. A thin ethereal melody that I knew I'd heard somewhere before in another life. Perhaps it was a product of my own mind, or perhaps a conduit between my mind and the insanity it had succumbed to. I cannot say for sure. I remember moving mutely forward as the singing filled my senses and the phantom absorbed me, digesting me until the Sam Cabot I had once known ewas gone.

A sudden and overwhelming panic gripped me as I writhed desperately in terror, trying to break free of the hideous bonds that now entrapped me. But it was too late. I *was* trapped, and I was suffocating, going down a spiral without end.

"Please know that the decision to offer your wife and only son as a sacrifice was the right one," the reaper said in a soft whisper that was nearly a snake-hiss. I jolted violently and felt pain in my mouth and wetness at my crotch. Dear God, it was me talking, not the reaper. Somehow I knew this to be true. The words were coming from my own hissing mouth! I'd seen them in the grave, I'd seen them burning in that terrible furnace, and it was I who had put them there; it was I who had led them here to this terrible place. I turned, still trapped helplessly in that body as I tried to run. It was like walking on the moon, moving underwater; my body was hot with fever, prickling with needles, my mind screaming in panic, screaming for release.

I came awake with a sudden wrenching jolt, as if I had just been shat from the bowels of Satan. I was in the living room chair, my body caught in the throes of violent convulsions. Blood ran down my chin. My tongue was wounded, bitten half off, my nightclothes were wet at the crotch as the unmistakable smell of shit wafted up from where I had soiled myself. I had fallen asleep as I'd contemplated the dream, only to be drawn back into its terrible embrace. I knew then what I had known and tried to deny since coming to Farnham House. Something had found me, something had *targeted* me, perhaps had even drawn me here, and I was not strong enough to resist its terrible persuasions. My wife! My son! I knew what had to be done! *I* had to do it or go mad. I had to do it or *die*.

After cleaning myself up, I went back upstairs and sat in the chair near my bed. I stared at Linda for a long time, the way her hair fell against the pillow, spreading out beneath her like a silk veil, the way her face shimmered in the dim moonlight from the window, so beautiful, so . . . innocent. I had never felt so helpless, so hopeless, so filled with despair. I got up and went to Sean's room, stood above his bed watching him sleep, afraid to touch him, afraid of what burned inside of me. I paced the floor for what seemed hours trying to puzzle out the nightmare, trying to find something in it that would give me a way out. But it was no good. Its intentions were clear. I *had* to succumb to the demons that had now fully invaded me. I had to or else. I had been receiving instructions for far too long to turn back now. The language was clear. The lesson was irrevocable. I stood in the hallway, doubled over with grief, wracked with convulsive sobs, my fists balled into helpless knots. Just before dawn, I went back down stairs, took the twelve gauge shotgun off the rack in the study, loaded it with ammo and stood at the foot of the stairwell for a long moment looking up, my finger twitching spasmodically as it caressed the trigger.

I turned and slipped out the back door and walked calmly toward the woods.

The wind was sharp and cold, quickly numbing my face, slowly numbing my body, then my senses. I liked it. Numb, I did not have to think or feel. I looked up and saw a billion stars, cold pinpoints of light in the darkness. Never in my life had the stars made me feel so completely small, so completely alone.

Chapter 20

I staggered out of the woods at dawn covered in soil and sweat and blood, the now ruined shotgun still clutched tightly in my blood-slicked hands. I have no memory of what happened out there. I'm still not sure. The circumstances that play out at the end of this story have convinced me of nothing. I may never know the real truth, and the simple truth is, I don't ever want to know.

I'd gone there fully intending to take my own life. But I could not do it. I'm not a coward, and I would have, except that thing inside me would not allow it. That left me with few choices. It made me realize there was only one way to stop the pain. I had to appease the reaper; it needed to be soon and I needed to be alive to do it.

I was back at the house, showered and had changed into clean clothes before Linda and Sean got out of bed. When they came down I had breakfast nearly ready.

I smiled and acted like everything was hunky dory. Linda poured a cup of coffee staring at me. "You can't keep doing this, Sam."

"Doing what?"

"You're kidding me, right?"

"No. I don't know what you mean."

Linda sighed. "You've got to let go."

"Let go?"

"Something's happened. We're not the same as we once were, you and me."

"Stop talking nonsense."

"It's not nonsense. Go look in the mirror."

"I don't want to," I said, discovering it nearly

impossible to speak around my swollen and bruised tongue.

"Afraid you might see the truth?"

"So, I had a bad night."

"That's a surprise."

"I bit my tongue,"

"There's blood and dirt all over the house. Jesus Christ, Sam."

"I'm okay now."

"Well *I'm* not okay, and neither is our son." Sean sat at the table his head cocked to the side resting in his hand, fidgeting with his Cheerios, acting like he wasn't hearing us.

"If you want to save your soul, you've got to stop," Linda said. "You've got to stop now."

"I . . . I'm . . . sorry," I said. "I don't know what's happening. It was just a bad dream."

"It was more than that, Sam. You think I'm stupid? You think I didn't know you weren't in bed for most of the night?" She stabbed her thumb toward the living room meaning she wanted a word with me in private. "We'll be back in a minute, Sean," she said. "Hurry up and eat your breakfast. You'll miss the school bus."

"I don't want to go to school, Mommy."

"What are you talking about? You always go to school."

"Not today. I'm scared."

Thoughts of chewing my ass gone, Linda went to our forlorn son and tenderly touched him, brushing the blond bangs out of his eyes. But something Linda had said a moment ago, perhaps unwittingly, persisted in my mind until I thought I'd go mad with it.

You've got to let go.

There was some hidden meaning there that I could

not grasp.

If you want to save your soul, you've got to stop.

Stop what? What was she trying to tell me? I watched her and Sean and felt a terrible aching in my heart. They were almost not real now, I could see right through them, like gauze; they were floating out beyond my reach, and I was drowning in a sea of despair.

"I had a bad dream last night," Sean said.

I stood beneath the archway between the kitchen and living room listening, suddenly wanting very much to know about Sean's dream.

"Do you want to talk about it?" Linda asked, her voice a gentle whisper.

Sean nodded. "I dreamed Mr. Carlisle was dead."

*

Linda shot me a terrified glance. "Listen, Sean, people have bad dreams all the time. Usually it's because they're worried about someone they care about. I think Mr. Carlisle's just fine. Don't you?"

No," Sean said in exasperation. "I don't mean he died. I mean he was already dead, a long time before we knew him. The man said he died and came back and that he needs other people to die so he can stay alive forever." Sean, staring fixedly into his untouched bowl of cereal began to weep.

"Jesus," Linda said scooping Sean up into her arms and hugging him close. She looked at me with wild eyes. Sean sobbed against her breast.

"What man, Sean?" I prodded, stepping back into the kitchen. I felt feverish suddenly, very much the way I'd felt in the dream just before melding with the reaper. "What man told you about Carlisle, son?"

"Stop it, Sam!" Linda snapped. "Jesus, isn't it bad enough?"

"I need to know, Linda!"

"The man with the mask," Sean sobbed.

"Christ," Linda breathed.

"Where did you see this man, Sean?"

"Shut up, Sam!" Linda screamed.

"Last night," Sean said. "He was in my bedroom. He was standing over my bed staring at me. He was wearing the green mask and he told me about Mr. Carlisle."

My jaw dropped, my eyes widened and I had to fight with everything inside me not to come completely unhinged. After waking up from that terrible two-part nightmare I had gone into Sean's room and watched him sleep. I remembered not daring to touch him, so afraid I might harm him. But somehow Sean had seen me as I truly was. How close had the monster I'd become come to . . . ? I didn't want to think about that, but I could not stop my mind.

"It's all right," Linda soothed, holding a sobbing Sean close. "Sean, you know it was just a dream, don't you. Mr. Carlisle is very much alive. I'll bet he'll even be here today. You understand that what I'm saying is true, don't you, son?"

"I guess so," Sean said listlessly.

Linda called the school and informed them that Sean was feeling a little under the weather and that in all likelihood he would be back at school tomorrow.

By nine o'clock, Linda had put him down for a nap. She said she thought he might be running a low-grade fever. She took his temperature and discovered that it was only slightly above normal, nothing to be concerned about yet. She stayed with him until his body fell into the rhythm of sleep. Then she tiptoed downstairs and stood facing me for a long time before speaking.

"Are you going fucking insane on me, Cabot? Is that what this is about?"

"I might be," I said, and surprisingly felt nothing. It was the first time I had ever actually voiced the thought and I felt nothing. That thing, the voice that wanted me to do unspeakable things could quite possibly be insanity, couldn't it? I reasoned. I hoped. At least in insanity my family might have a chance. They could put me away. Lock me up and throw away the key.

NO! YOU MUST NOT THINK SUCH THOUGHTS, this sudden and very powerful voice spoke up inside me, wanting to drive me to my knees. I tried to still it, but it would not be bullied. My head began to throb with the effort. I put my hands on either side of it hoping to hold it together.

WE HAVE COME TOO FAR TO TURN BACK NOW!

My heart was pounding madly. I felt wetness on my chin and touched it with my fingertips. It was blood, of course, dripping from my mouth, and now from my nose.

"Christ," Linda said, running for the kitchen sink. She wet a cloth and put it on my face, washing the blood away. "You're sick, Sam. I want you to see a doctor."

"I don't need a—"

"Bull shit! Look at you. You're a scarecrow, all bones. There are hollows in your cheeks and your eyes are rimmed in black. You're *sick!* Something's eating you away, and if you don't do something about it I will."

"Okay," I said, holding my hands up defensively. "I'll call the doctor."

"Promise?"

"I'll do it today."

Linda watched me without emotion. "I need some answers."

"I don't have any."

"I think you do, Sam. You're scaring the shit out of me."

"I'm sorry."

"And Carlisle scares me too."

"What?"

"I just get a bad feeling when he's around. Maybe now that the place is all fixed up he'll go away. God only knows what kind of baggage a man like that carries around with him. He certainly doesn't confide in either of us." Linda burst suddenly into tears. I did not dare touch her although my heart yearned to. She stood facing me, tears running down her cheeks. "Sam, please, I'm worried about Sean. He's so taken with Carlisle. I see him following him around all the time talking his ear off. Is it possible that Carlisle tells him things that aren't meant for a six-year-old?"

"What things?"

"You heard what Sean just said. Christ, I don't know, but I'm telling you he's freaking me out. I was in the basement the other day looking over that old chest of drawers down there, checking to see if it was salvageable, and from out of nowhere Carlisle comes up behind me and scares the living shit out of me. In this short and impatient voice he asked me what I was doing down there. In my own basement. Can you believe that? I was so startled that I caught myself explaining to him and feeling like an intruder. I don't know what he was doing in there, but suddenly I got a really bad vibe from him."

"Probably checking on the heating plant, you know how he feels about that thing."

"Yes, I do. He fixed it, and he paid for it, and sometimes . . . I don't know. Sometimes I feel like he's using it . . . against us . . . in some weird way. Jesus, I don't know."

She came into my arms then, sobbing. I did not know what to do. I stood rigid and did not hug her back. She didn't seem real anymore. I couldn't feel her. I nearly couldn't see her.

"Maybe we should borrow the money and pay him in full for the house. Maybe then he would get out of our lives."

"I doubt he'd take it," I said, and felt numb. I was just going through the motions, trying to appease her.

"Well, what are we going to do then?"

"I don't know."

"I need to get away from here, Sam. I need to get Sean away from here. Just for a little while. Do you think we could go somewhere for the Thanksgiving holiday?" Her voice was almost pleading. "Maybe that would give us a fresh perspective on things."

I didn't answer her right away. I didn't know if I would actually be allowed to leave this place. That thing I had become a part of, or that had become a part of me, did not like what I was contemplating. I licked my lips, staring at Linda, knowing that she deserved an answer. "Okay," I said finally, not sure if it was the truth or a lie. "We'll go."

Chapter 21

There was snow in the air. The sky was low and gunmetal gray, the temperature hovering at around the thirty degree mark. I spent the remainder of the afternoon working between the basement and the yard, enjoying fall's sharp bite, cleaning up and storing stuff away for the impending winter; rakes, shovels, water hoses, lawn mower and gas cans. It was good being outside in the briskness of a November day. It brought back fond memories of long ago; deer hunting with my father, coming back into a warm and friendly kitchen, all out of breath and tingly with excitement, the smell of supper cooking on the stove. How good those times had been. Dear God, how much I missed them. Now it felt like the memories belonged to someone else. It couldn't possibly have been me who had lived in those times, done all those things. Oh how their loss had devastated me, left me emotionally and physically drained for so very long. They'd been on their way home from a New Year's Eve party . . . Dad's blood alcohol level had been off the charts. The policeman standing at the door with his hat in his hand and a solemn look on his face . . . so sudden . . . so unfair . . . never got the chance to say goodbye; the policemen holding me back; *please, Mr. Cabot, there's nothing you can do . . . they're gone.*

I jolted violently. The memory of the night they'd died and the terrible dreams I'd been experiencing since coming to this house had somehow fused together. I no longer knew which parts were real, which were nightmares.

Ever since that day, I'd been totally incapable of demonstrating any kind of closeness. No wonder

Linda and I had grown apart. It could all end and I'd be in that place again.

It has ended. You just haven't accepted it yet.

You've got to let go, Sam.

The grief multiplied suddenly, taking me to some unthinkable place, some terrible knowledge.

Since coming to this house I'd been on a downward spiral, this was irrefutable; bent on a mission of self-destruction, but more than that, drawn by a force beyond my control, I was actually contemplating my family's destruction. But *was* it beyond my control? Could Linda be right? Maybe I *was* sick, mentally or emotionally sick in the way people who are institutionalized are sick. So many questions. Jesus, so many blank spots.

*

Carlisle didn't come on that day and it was sort of a relief, it gave me time to think about things in a way I hadn't in a long while, and it felt good. In the basement, I tried my best to avoid the Hulk's grisly seductions.

Chapter 22

Carlisle showed up the following day, late in the afternoon, riding that red and chrome fat-wheeled 1950s bicycle up the drive toward the house. I watched through the living room window. He was bundled up in an old gray parka, a scarf around his neck and a wool cap on his head. I wondered how he did it; a man his age, riding all that distance this late in the year with an icy wind ushering in the promise of snow. There was something mysterious and almost supernatural about him. The thought had crossed my mind many times during the summer that things just weren't right with Carlisle. The things I'd heard, the things I'd seen. The things he'd said to me. His only interest seemed to be this old house. Then an intriguing thought struck me. His interest wasn't actually the house. He rarely came inside, only when we'd insisted, for lunch or a cold drink which he rarely touched. He would comment only generally and with little interest, it seemed, as to our progress in restoring the place. No, his only real interest here was and always had been the heating system. The two were connected in some twisted and terrible way.

I was putting on my coat, intending to go outside and have a little heart-to-heart with the old man when the phone rang.

"Linda," I called. "I'm going outside to speak with Carlisle. Would you please get the phone?" It rang again. "Linda?" She must have been in another part of the house. Sean had come home from school again feeling out of sorts and she'd put him down for a nap.

You've got to let go, Sam.

The thought nearly paralyzed me.

Perhaps she was napping with him. I picked up the phone and John said, "You got a minute, Sam?"

"I just put my coat on. I was headed outside to speak with Carlisle."

"That's what I wanted to talk to you about."

"Carlisle? Really? What about?"

"You remember back early in the summer how me and Carlisle got to be sort of friendly?"

"Yeah."

"You remember how after a while that friendship soured? How I began to distrust him?"

"Sure, I remember that too. What's this about, John?"

"Well, he told me he lived down by the town pier."

"Yeah, that's what he told us, too."

"Well, he lied."

"How do you know that?" I walked over to the window, pulled the curtain aside and looked out. Carlisle was no longer in view. He must have already gone into the basement.

I waited in anticipation, unable to stop the shiver that trickled down my back. I continued to stare out the kitchen window at the front yard. The shadows of the barren trees that lined the yard angled across the down-sloping lawn like pointed teeth. Deeper in the woods the shadows seemed denser, almost as if they had an existence of their own, separate from the forest around them.

"Well, he never would give me an address," John went on, "so I had Meg drive me down to the pier and I checked around and nobody down there knows anything about him."

"There must be some mistake," I said. "Linda gave him a ride home once . . . last . . . summer." My voice faltered. As I was mouthing the words I knew something wasn't quite right. My memory of that incident and the terrible dreams I'd had that day didn't add up. I could not honestly remember Linda ever speaking of that day, or Carlisle, or where she'd taken him, after she'd gotten home. Why hadn't I asked her where Carlisle lived?

I stumbled away from the window and fell into a chair. The trembling in my body had worsened. My brow was covered in a cold, slick sheen of sweat. "What do you mean, nobody knows anything about him?"

"Sam . . . Listen. When I mention him, folks just get these blank looks on their faces, like they're confused or something. Some say they haven't laid eyes on him in years. Others have only vague memories of him. Most never heard of him. Several people I talked to told me he's been dead for at least half a century."

"Dead?" I said choking out a hoarse laugh. "That's impossible."

"I know," John replied. "That's what I said. Sam, the truth is, he never lived down by the pier."

"Well, where does he live then?" I could hear my voice rising in panic.

"I don't really have an answer for that, Sam, but I can tell you what I think."

"Yes, John, why don't you tell me what you think?"

"I think he lives there at the house."

"Carlisle? This house?" My voice was filled with incredulity. "What the hell are you talking about?"

"That's his legal address, Sam. The one he's used since 1944, since he went off and joined the Merchant Marine. That's his family home, you know. He grew up there."

"Yes, I know, but Jesus Christ, he doesn't live here now."

"I think he does, Sam."

"John, make sense."

"I did some further digging. I went to the town office and checked and the place is still listed in his name."

"That can't be," I said. "We signed papers. Money was exchanged. I have a mortgage."

"Are you absolutely sure about that, Sam?"

"Of course I'm sure! We had a lawyer draw up the papers."

"What Layer?"

"A lawyer in town. You remember, don't you, John?"

"Sam, I remember you and Linda telling us that you were *going* to have a lawyer draw up the papers. Last time I talked to my daughter she said that it hadn't been done yet. She said that you kept making excuses."

"That's not true, John."

"Isn't it, Sam?"

"*Goddammit*, John, if the house is still in Carlisle's name and he's been dead fifty years, then who's paying the damned taxes?"

"I asked at the town office and they said the money comes from an escrow account. They tap it once a year and don't ask questions."

"What the hell's going on, John?"

"You tell me."

"How should I know?"

"Listen, Sam, there's something else." I noticed that John's voice had gotten a little hoarse.

"What, John? Jesus Christ, what is it?"

"First, I want you to promise me you'll get the hell

out of that evil house before it's too late. Me and Meg still care very much about you, you know."

"You mean get out now?"

"Yes, now."

"Whatever for, John? Tell me! And what do you mean, you and Meg still care very much about me?"

"Listen carefully, Sam. I got on the Internet and did some checking. I punched in the name Francis J. Carlisle and found out that an ancestor of his with the same name came over from England with William Farnham, the original owner, in the early eighteenth century. He was Farnham's builder and handyman."

"Yes, I've heard that before, from a neighbor."

"And you didn't say anything?"

"I didn't think it was important."

"Listen to me, Sam. Another man with the name Francis J. Carlisle died in a fire at Farnham house in 1850. That's what the records show. That would have been about a hundred and fifty years after Farnham and the original Carlisle came here."

"Maybe it was the original Carlisle's grandson or great-grandson."

"I don't think so, Sam."

"What are you saying, John?" Are you telling me that the original Carlisle never actually died? That he's gone through life occasionally faking his own death so as not to draw suspicion? Are you telling me that he's somehow still alive and he's the Carlisle we know?"

"I can't answer that, Sam. I only know what I found on the internet. I checked further and looked up some old service records from the Second World War. Most of those old records are in the public domain now. Again I punched in the name Francis J. Carlisle and a man by that name with *your* address came up. The ship he was on, the *Santa Rosa,* it was an old cargo ship taken over by the Navy to be used for re-supplying Navy warships on duty in the North Atlantic. Well, the *Santa Rosa* was torpedoed by a German sub and it went down with all hands listed as lost. Carlisle was listed as missing in action."

I was gasping for breath now. Sean's dream of Carlisle being dead came back to me with breathtaking reality and I wanted to scream. "But Carlisle is *alive,*" I told John, wanting very much to put a rational face on the situation. "He's flesh and blood. I've shaken his hand. I've had drinks with him. So have you. He's *alive,* isn't he, John?"

"Sam, whatever that thing is that calls itself Carlisle isn't a man."

"What the hell are you talking about?" I *was* on the verge of screaming now.

"Sam, me and Meg are really worried about you. We're in the car. We'll be there in twenty minutes."

"But, why?"

"We're getting you out of that place. This has gone on too long."

"Jesus, John, what has gone on too long?"

Sam, you've got to let go.

"Your denial, Sam."

"Denial?"

"They're gone, Sam. You've got to accept that. And I think Carlisle might have had something to do with it."

"Gone?" I said. "Who's gone?" There was silence on the line and now the despair was dragging on me like a tide, imploding from within, pulling me down like bad gravity.

"Sam, you've got to stop living your life like they're

still there."

"Linda and Sean? Is that who you're talking about? Because they're here, John, you bet your ass they are! Sean's upstairs taking a nap and Linda's doing laundry or something."

"Sam . . . you're being irrational."

"Irrational?" I screamed, knowing in my heart of hearts that I was kidding myself. Hell, I was being more than irrational, I was planning on giving my wife and child up as burnt offerings so an old man who refused to die, an old man—hell, a monster—who'd lived a hundred lifetimes, could live another lifetime or two. What the hell was I thinking? I bolted from my chair and ran back to the window. It was nearly dark now and the skeletal trees beyond the driveway now looked like tombstones in some lost and forlorn graveyard. I could see that snow was falling in thick squalls. Carlisle's bike still rested against the shed, only now it no longer looked all shiny and new; now it was rusted and ruined, the tires were flat and in places, large pieces of rubber were actually missing, rotted away like cancerous tumors. Brown weeds grew up against its rusted frame like dead flowers on the face of some macabre cemetery marker. My heart lurched and nearly stopped. I threw the phone down, hearing John screaming for me to pick it up. I ran to the stairs and called up for Linda and Sean. When there was no answer, I took the stairs two at a time and bolted down the hallway slamming open doors as I went. They were not in our room; they were not in Sean's room, nor were they in any other of the upstairs rooms. Dear God, where were they? But I knew. Jesus Christ and all that is sane, I *knew*. As I dashed back down the stairs I heard Linda screaming on the other end of the phone, very loud and very clear. *". . . someone in the road . . . get out of the way! Oh, dear God, Sam! What are you doing here? Can't control . . ."* I heard the insane shrieking of tires on pavement, Linda's stifled scream, a horrendous crash and then silence.

I stared mutely at the phone in my hand, my eyes wide with horror. Had I heard correctly? She'd seen me there at the site of the crash. But I couldn't have been there. I was asleep on the couch having a terrible dream when the . . . accident . . . happened.

There's blood on your feet. They're all scraped and scratched. No, this can't be.

I grabbed the phone back up. "Linda?" I said, my voice choked with emotion. "Is that you, baby?"

"It's me, Sam," John said. "Get out of that house while you still can."

"How many people died in that wreck, John? Goddammit, *tell me now!*"

"There were only two of them in the car, Sam. Linda and Sean."

"But Carlisle went with them that day."

"He might've gone with them, Sam. But when the cops got there it was just Linda and Sean."

Chapter 23

For the longest time I could not breathe, frozen as I was in complete and utter horror. When my numb body finally allowed me the luxury of movement I dumped the phone out of my hand and began a systematic search of the downstairs rooms, but knew in my true heart where I would find Linda and Sean. I had never in my life dreaded any moment more than I did that one. I opened the cellar door and the blast hit me like a barrage of hot wind, yanking the door from my grasp and slamming it against the wall. I faced the hot wind and began my descent into hell. There was no need for me to carry a light; the basement was a hive of it, pulsing with every known color of the spectrum and probably some that did not belong in this universe.

At that moment I had no more control over my destiny than an insect does beneath a descending shoe. My hands held my head, a slight throbbing already beginning at the base of my spine and moving up into my brain until I thought it would explode, but this did not deter me. My mind said scream, but more profoundly my mind said do not falter, and in complete contrast to what my mind said, my entire being urged me to flee the sickness, flee all that lived within the confines of Farnham House, all that was *true*, all that had conspired to ruin three promising lives. Get away. *Dear, God, get away while you still can.* Then the music came; thin, ethereal, alien, but *alive*, and the resolve fled.

I was lost.

Turning right at the foot of the stairs I walked trance-like to the workbench. I searched behind it for the mask, but it was not there. I reached up and touched my face and realized for the first time that I'd been wearing it since the awful day Linda and Sean went away, only to return as ghosts. I understood this quite clearly now in that subterraneous place that felt deeper than the gaping hole in my heart.

I turned back around, and came face to face with dozens of shadow people, their glittering eyes shining like angry stars in an alien night sky. They'd been there from the beginning, of course, watching me, waiting, biding their time. I suspected who they were; the souls of those who had, in one way or another, crossed paths with the thing that called itself Francis Carlisle. They were his collection, his bidders, his puppets, his toys. He'd taken them and they'd gone willingly. They were a necessary part of his evolution, just like I was, just like Linda and Sean were. Without giving them another thought I pushed through their ranks, their diaphanous bodies parting like smoke in a brisk wind.

With slow deliberateness I moved toward the source of the frenetic light. The corpses of Linda and Sean lay placid on their backs near the Hulk's fiery maw. They were partially decayed and horribly misshapen, covered in grave dirt. A thing that might have been Francis Carlisle stood over them holding a machete.

"We've been waiting," it said and smiled. I saw the creature's true self then, appalling in its grotesquery, like it had come from someplace beyond this earth; perhaps beyond the dim recesses of time. The eyes were bright white and soulless orbs sunk deeply into bruise-colored sockets. The teeth in its head belonged more in the mouth of a shark. It had no hair; the elongated skull shown wet like it had just slid from the blackness of some cosmic womb; the ears were those of a bat. It wore no clothes; the body was thin, emaciated, the color of spoiled milk. No sex was evident, but I guessed that creatures such as this had no use for sex organs. "I see you understand the rules," it said, gesturing toward the mask on my face.

I nodded, looking down at my dead loved ones, then back at their unmaker. "What are you?" I said.

"You haven't guessed by now?"

"Just tell me."

"I am nothing and everything. I am the negative and the positive, the darkness and the light. I am your biggest fear and your greatest hope. I am the air that you breathe, the food that you eat and the waste that you shit."

"Why me?" I said. "Why my family?"

"Oh, dear boy. You wanted this as much as I did. You *chose* this."

I shook my head. "No," I said. "You're lying."

"Oh but you did. Think back, Sammy-boy. Remember the details."

I pointed at the Hulk's fiery maw. "What does that have to do with this?"

"Everything."

"You bastard! You killed them, then you dug them up?"

The Carlisle-thing shook its head. "No," it said. "You did that to them. All by yourself. You destroyed them, and then *you* brought them back."

"But why would I destroy the two people I love most in the world?"

"Because you love something else even more."

"I don't care what you say. Nothing will ever make be believe I did that to them."

"Suit yourself, Sam. It doesn't matter now. What does matter is that you remember the details. Think back. Do you recall the Bashgal Valley of Afghanistan? How you were on your way to help your brothers in arms? They'd been flushing out caves along the ridges there looking for Taliban fighters when they were ambushed."

"Yes, of course I remember, but what does it have to do with any of this?"

"Everything, Sam. Think about it. A rat came up out of a hole and shot your helicopter down. You were the only survivor."

"I was lucky."

The Carlisle thing chuckled. "No, my dear boy, you weren't lucky you were *chosen*."

"Chosen? For what?"

"For this very moment in time. You see, you only remembered part of what happened that day. You were so afraid of death you would have done anything to survive. But you wanted much more than life and I was there to oblige."

"Is that what this is about?" I said. "Some kind of twisted version of the Devil and Daniel Webster? Because if it is I don't believe it."

"Of course you don't, but you soon will. I promise."

I searched back in my mind. The crash I had always remembered, of course, like a malignant tumor at the center of my being. I was sitting there with the other soldiers, my friends, men I depended on, my mind numb with the realization that I would soon be thrust again into the heat of combat where in the blink of an eye a bullet could end everything. And then the explosion of metal and glass and warm body parts as the floor was pulled out from under me, and what was left of the helicopter plunged toward something large and dark and without meaning, down through concentric circles, going round and round, dizzying, faster, circle after circle, a jumble of blurred faces, cries of pain, grunts of fear and anguish, and darkness, round and round . . . into the abyss.

The rest of what happened that day had always eluded me.

But now I was starting to remember.

It seemed a long time before I regained consciousness. I was nowhere near the crash site, which by now was nothing more than a smoking pile of rubble that nothing could have escaped from. There was pain in my elbow, and I was mutely aware of the burns on my hands and face.

I wandered until I came to a series of hills. But they weren't just hills, they were different somehow, in a way that I could not explain then and can only vaguely describe now. They were like nothing I had ever seen before, demented, deformed, not of this world. A thin humanoid figure stood atop one of the craggy hills beckoning. More hills broke the distant horizon. And there were flames rising up between them, a pall of smoke and ash, the air so thick and dense I almost could not breathe.

I knew in that moment that I was in hell.

Chapter 24

"You remember now, don't you, Sam?" the Carlisle thing said, bringing me back to the present.

"But I don't remember why," I said.

"Oh, you mean the bargain. You still don't see?"

I shook my head.

"What is it you have always dreaded, Sam? What has always frightened you most in life? It is the danger of being overlooked. Of being irrelevant. Of being just another face in the crowd. Isn't that true? I heard your call and came to your rescue. I got you out of that fiery wreck and offered you what you could not get anywhere else. I offered you what was only a dream until that moment: immortality. Now it is time for you to finish what we started." Carlisle proffered the machete. "You need to feed the fire."

"Why?"

"Because that's the way it's done, the way it's been done since the beginning of time. We have always fed the fire."

Suddenly my entire being, mind, body and soul convulsed as if I'd grabbed hold of a live electric wire. And finally I remembered everything.

*

I'm not sure how long I stood there in hell just staring at those strange burning hills, but eventually I stumbled up the rocky incline toward the beckoning figure on the ledge. There were many cave openings beneath the strange burning hills and I imagined enemy soldiers hiding out in them using their sanctuary to plot war crimes. I didn't care. Out of exhaustion I followed the figure into the nearest opening. What I had at first thought was a small cave opened up into a vast stone chamber bathed in flickering light. Black candles were set in sconces along both sides of the chamber's rough stone walls. In the center of the chamber there sat a long table of dark wood with more flickering black candles, these set into silver holders. Ancient looking high-backed chairs surrounded the table. The chairs were all occupied by human figures dressed in red robes and cowls. In the flickering light their faces were pallid gray shadows inside the cowls and I could not make out any detail. On the table, in front of each of the robed figures, sat a crystal goblet filled with red liquid. The room was rich with the smell of hazel incense. A quartz sphere was placed at the center of the table.

It was obvious that this was a place of ritual. A massive throne, much larger than the chairs surrounding the table, dominated the far end of the chamber. It was impossible to tell what the throne was constructed of for it looked like nothing of this earth; its surface scaly, leather-like, and it seemed to grow and shrink in an even cadence, as though it was alive and breathing.

On the whitewashed stone wall behind the throne a large symbol was emblazoned in black.

I had no idea what that symbol represented. I still

don't. Perhaps I never will. A figure clad in black robes sat motionless on the throne. Its face was impossible to discern, for the hood cast it in shadow. The only things I could see clearly were two glittering red eyes.

"Who are you?" I asked. "What do you want?"

"Step closer."

I hesitated a moment too long.

"STEP CLOSER!"

"I had no choice but to obey. Its will was greater than mine. I stepped to the end of the long table as the men around it picked up their glasses and began to chant in a language I did not recognize. Then they all upended their goblets at once and drank down the red liquid within.

On the throne the black robe catapulted into the air, over the man's head, and he was lifted by the force of it, by a flapping wave that carried him above the long table. The robe flew into streaming pennants that became muscular wings flapping slowly in the hot air, crackling with static electricity which whipped across the great cavern like bolts of lightning, bringing into focus the lurid faces of the seated figures. And that's when I saw that they were not men but monsters.

And then a face appeared as the hovering figure's cowl slipped. It was not human, nor was it a bat or a bird, but something perhaps not of this earth, something that came from a place back in the dim beginnings of time. Red darting eyes fixed on me, holding me in their thrall. It gazed at me as it rowed the air with its black leathery wings.

*

"I remember now," I said to the Carlisle thing. "I

agreed to give you something that didn't even exist then. Linda and I weren't married and a child wasn't even on the radar. What would be the harm?"

"Exactly," said the Carlisle thing.

"But why the middle of Afghanistan?"

"Easy pickings. Human suffering. Death. War is where I do my best work. Lots of bargains to be made."

Linda and Sean began to animate, their eyes opening.

The Carlisle thing gestured toward them. "Their souls will soon be mine. But first they need to burn."

I began to see at least part of what was happening here. Most of it would always elude me, of course. There are things that live at the very fringes of the universe, terrible yet true things that mortal man must never delve too deeply into, lest he risk lunacy. How could I have bargained with the souls of those I loved most? What kind of monster was I? How could I have lived all these months thinking my family was alive when they were just ghosts, or worse, a figment of some terrible madness? This *was* madness, of course. There could be no other explanation. There never had been any devil bargaining for souls. It was all in my head. *This* was all in my head. I was as nutty as a fruit cake.

Even so, it all looked and felt real. I could see that the corpses were trying to rise now; loose, wet sacks of putrefaction.

Carlisle proffered the machete. "You need to finish the job," he said. "You need to feed the fire."

I shook my head. "Never!"

"You must."

The Hulk roared loudly in frustration, tongues of

flame licking out through the door's louvers. It was hungry for them. I could see that. And I was supposed to do the deed. I was supposed to feed them to that thing.

Linda and Sean had managed somehow to stand and they were watching me longingly with blank, wet eyes. "This can't be," I said. "They're dead. Look at them." They began lurching toward me, zombies from the grave.

"No," said Carlisle, coming between me and them. "Not dead. Not alive. But you'll be dead if you don't take this. It's what they want. Don't you see? It's the only way they can . . . live again."

"Live again?" I said, a feeling of hot and terrible hope swelling inside me.

"You'd like to have them back, wouldn't you?"

"But how?"

"Just do it and you will see."

I reached up to pull the mask off my face and discovered that there was no mask there. Had there ever been? "You son of a bitch," I said. "You tricked me!"

"Are you sure about that?" Carlisle replied with a terrible laugh. "Do you know what's real and what isn't?"

He was right, of course. I didn't have a fucking clue. Six months and it had all been illusion; now more of the same. I was supposed to believe that my wife and son had died and been resurrected so that they could die again, and thus be resurrected for a second time, this time by my own hand so that this creature who lived on the souls of others could continue to live. I was supposed to take the machete from him, cut them up and feed them to that thing, so that it could live, so that *they* could live again in some corrupt and hellish existence.

"What about the thing in the well?" I said. "What about Devlin? Was *any* of it real?"

"What do you think, Sam?" Carlisle's shark tooth studded mouth shaped itself into a terrible expression that might have been a grin. He made a gesture with his hand and several of the foundation's fieldstones broke free and crashed to the earthen floor. From the crevice slid a creature I could not in a million years have fathomed. I knew immediately, however, that it was the same creature that had taken the life of a young man named Devlin, a man who had threatened the status quo by his very presence on this cursed property.

It was some sort of serpent, or reptile, or both, but neither somehow. Like Carlisle, it was something not of this earth. Its skin was scaly and mottled, its eyes glittering blood-rubies. It wound itself around Carlisle's frail form like a boa constrictor embracing its trusting handler.

"Jesus Christ," I mouthed, backing away. "Oh, Jesus Christ." Again the Carlisle thing shaped its terrible grin.

Linda and Sean were moaning and writhing as they lurched toward me. They could not stay whole for much longer, this was clear, for the corruption was far too advanced. Chunks of flesh were sliding off them and splashing to the floor. I was having trouble holding onto what thin strands of sanity I had left. The serpent, or whatever the hell it was, had lifted its head from Carlisle and was inching toward me, its blood-ruby eyes curious yet hostile. I saw needle-pointed fangs protruding from its upper jaw as its mouth began to open. It was sniffing, taking my scent.

"Take it, and do it!" the Carlisle thing said, once again proffering the machete, shaking it at me with urgency and anger. "They'll be remade in the conflagration. I promise you it is so."

"You do it," I said. "If you're what you say you are then you don't need me."

"Oh, but I do. You need to do it for them to live!"

I was backed into a corner now, as far as I could go. I glanced down and saw the gas can I'd stored there yesterday. I could not think straight, but I needed to. "What is that thing?" I said, pointing at the creature, trying to buy more time.

"You like?" Carlisle seemed to brighten a little.

I nodded as the serpent's head and upper torso came closer, its powerful muscles rippling as it did so. It was inspecting me like food.

"Something I found in the sea," Carlisle said. "Or perhaps it found me. It promised to be a good companion. And it has more than lived up to my expectations."

"Keeps the nosy away, eh?"

Carlisle nodded slightly.

"You died on that ship, didn't you?"

"Died?" Carlisle said as if the idea was preposterous. "I needed to feed the fire, that's all. They were many and I was one. I told you, war is where I do my best work. I was discretionary. What's the loss of one sailor or soldier every now and then, especially in wartime? Some make bargains, most don't. When the torpedo struck I watched them burn. And I fed the fire."

The thing that had been my son began moving jerkily around Carlisle and his companion. The places where his eyes had once been were milk-white pools. Linda moved around his other side. She put her hand out to me in a gesture of supplication. Her decayed lips moved and I wanted to die because I knew what she was trying to say. She needed me to end their suffering. *"Please?"* her lips begged. *"Please, do it now, Sam."* One of her legs collapsed and she went down in a heap, only to pull herself along the earthen floor toward me with dead fingers, her rotted lips still mouthing silent exclamations.

Behind them the Hulk roared mightily, shooting licks of flame from its terrible maw. The reptile thing struck suddenly, but I feinted and it missed. Poisonous fluid sprayed from its fangs, hissing like acid on contact with the floor.

"If it kills me then what'll you do?" I said.

"That was a warning." Carlisle said, his mad, sunken eyes flaming with hate. "Take it to heart for it was your last." He held the machete out to me. "You *must* do it! It's the only way."

The Hulk was roaring almost constantly now.

"Fuck you," I said. The serpent struck a second time. It was expecting me to feint again, but I didn't. As its head shot past me I stepped forward and snatched the machete from Carlisle's hand, swinging it powerfully over my head and bringing the blade down onto the serpent's neck, severing its head cleanly. Caustic yellow fluid sprayed from its severed appendage like boiling acid.

An agonizing cry wrenched from the Carlisle thing's throat as the creature fell away from him in two parts and began writhing on the floor. I brought the machete down again, this time on the gasoline can at my feet, nearly cutting it in two. I picked it up and tossed a sheet of the flammable liquid across Carlisle, my wife, and my son. The Hulk roared its approval, sending out a tongue of fire that tasted the fuel.

I don't remember much after that, just bits and pieces that make no sense when I try to put them into context. I was blown back against the door with such force I nearly lost consciousness. I remember being on fire watching everything burn, happy that it was over, happy that I was burning too.

Epilogue

When I awoke in the hospital, John and Meg were there. I watched them watch me for a long moment.

"How are you feeling?" Meg asked.

"I don't know." I tried to move, but couldn't. There were bandages on my hands and around my torso. I couldn't feel my legs. "How bad is it?"

"You'll live," said John.

"You should have left me there."

Meg gave a helpless look. "Why do you say that, Sam?"

"They're gone," I said and felt tears flood my eyes.

"It was that terrible house," John said. "You never should have bought it. You never should have trusted that evil man."

"How did I get out?"

"We arrived just after the fire started. It took both of us to drag you out. I wasn't much help. Mostly Meg did it."

I looked at Meg. "You saw them then."

"Saw . . . who, Sam?"

My probing eyes went from Meg to John, then back to Meg. "They were *there*," I said. "In the cellar."

"Sam," John began, and then his voice faltered. "Listen . . . ever since the accident we've been trying to reach you. You refused to believe they were gone. Something . . . maybe it was that house, I don't know, but something would not allow us to get near you, the same thing that wouldn't allow you to accept what had happened."

"That they were dead?" I said, now breaking into heavy sobs.

"Yes," said Meg. "During and after the funeral you

were too numb to react. We understood so we left you alone. You went home. John called two days later and you got in a big fight. You said that Linda and Sean were there with you and that you were doing just fine. You wouldn't talk to us after that; you wouldn't take our calls. When we came by you locked the doors and wouldn't let us in. We know how much you loved them, Sam. We loved them too." Meg wept.

"But they were *there*," I insisted, and I could feel my blood heating up and my eyes widening with emotion. "John . . . Jesus Christ, you have to believe me. After I talked to you on the phone and I finally realized what had happened, I went down into the basement, because I knew they would be there. And I was right. Carlisle had dug them up—only he said I did it—and he'd put them in front of the heating system, and I was supposed to cut them up and feed them to that thing." My voice faltered when I saw the pitying looks on their faces.

"There was nobody in that basement but you, Sam," Meg said.

"But—"

"Nobody," John said.

I closed my hot wet eyes, knowing that it was useless. They were probably right. I was sick and it had all been some terrible hallucination. "The house?" I said.

"We let it burn," John said with satisfaction. "All the way to the ground. Never even called the fire department."

"And good riddance to it," Meg added with a shudder of revulsion.

"Carlisle?"

John's expression was one I could not pigeonhole.

It might have been fear or anger or relief. Or all of the above. To this day I'm not sure. "No one's seen him since before the place burned."

I started to speak, but John stopped me. "He wasn't in the house, Sam. Any more than he was in the car that day with Linda and Sean. You can get those notions out of your head right now. After the fire went out they combed every inch of that place. You were the only living thing in there."

What about dead things? I wondered, but did not voice the thought. How could they ever understand that I'd been living with dead things all those months? "How did the fire start?" I said instead.

John and Meg both looked uncomfortable.

"You did it, Sam, and we thank God you finally found the courage to torch that place. Meg and I took care of the evidence. It's been listed as an accident. They think that old monster of a heating system blew up. Never did like that thing much. Something about it always gave me the creeps, if you want the truth."

I swallowed thickly and stared at John. "Yeah, me too," I said.

*

It took me years to get past the events of that summer. How could one man go so utterly beyond reason that he didn't even notice his family had slipped beyond his grasp?

Eventually I healed, physically at least, and in time I got my rhythm back and began writing again. The rest you know. I became a big success, translating grief into art. John has since passed on. Meg still lives in the same place in town. I haven't seen her in years. I never told anyone about what really happened here that summer, and as far as I know, neither did they. The secret died with John. And now I have to make sure it dies with Meg.

Now, as I stand here on this worn old path staring down into a watery abyss, things are starting to become a little clearer in my mind. You see, I had an ulterior motive for coming back here after all these years. I wanted to feel the place out, see if I could handle my emotions. And to tell you the truth, I think I'm going to be okay. Lately I've been thinking seriously about building a new house over the old foundation. Perhaps I'll open an inn. I'll call it Farnham House. Why change the name? The old sign is still out on the gate. Who knows, maybe I'll even get the Hulk up and running again. So, I guess I should be getting back to town. My new wife and son are waiting for me at the hotel there.

I know they're anxious to hear what I've decided.

Wonder if Carlisle is still around?

THE END

About The Author

Mark Edward Hall is the author of twenty books, including the bestselling novel Apocalypse Island, the first book in the Blue Light Series. Soul Thief, the second book in the Blue Light Series is out now.

Mark enjoys writing, reading, fishing, playing guitar, singing and spending time at camp in the Maine woods with his wife, Sheila. He lives in Maine and Florida.

In the third book of the Blue Light Series Doug and Annie McArthur are forced to take refuge in the Maine Wilderness. Ariel has grown into a beautiful and gifted child wise beyond her years. Their life, although hard, has been peaceful and relatively quiet. But the tide is about to turn. When they sense something isn't right in the world Doug leaves the shelter of their wilderness cabin to investigate. In a heartbeat their quiet life is shattered by an unspeakable violence, and once again they are forced to run for their lives, this time to a place where they will encounter a truth more fantastic than anything they could ever have imagined. Here, in a world turned upside down by evil they will have to find the courage to let their only child go, for she is the chosen one, the only person on earth capable of venturing into the darkness beyond the Blue Light where salvation for the human race might or might not await.

Please turn the page for a sneak preview of

Song of Ariel

Prologue

Burbank, Texas 11:59 pm July 3rd the day of the arrival.

Leroy Parks solemnly locked the door of the quick stop precisely at midnight. Tonight traffic on the boulevard was uncharacteristically light. The quick stop sat next to Interstate 90 on the edge of the dusty desert town of Burbank, Texas USA, halfway between nothing and nowhere. Business was bad, worse than Leroy had ever seen. Gas and diesel prices were at an all-time high and though he knew folks had to fill up, he suspected some were stretching what they had in their tanks for as long as possible. All night long, over on the highway, trucks and cars droned past without stopping. Ah, well, he thought bitterly, life sucks then you die.

The only place along the strip with any real activity was across the boulevard at the Dunes Diner. People had to eat. That was the truth. And tonight the Dunes looked like it had more than its share of hungry patrons.

Leroy worked for the man. His quick stop was part of a chain, just one of a little million of them scattered all over the southwest, and although he was the manager, his salary was low, benefits were barely adequate, and it was a struggle getting by. The only light at the end of the tunnel was Wendy. He'd go home and crawl in bed with her, feel the warmth of her body as she spooned her buttocks against him, and he would dream about the two of them escaping to some tropical island where they would both live happily ever after.

But by the time Leroy made it across the lot to his pickup truck all thoughts of Wendy and happily-ever-after had fled from his mind.

The Night Wind had begun to blow . . .

. . . Leroy took a few robust whiffs of it, liked its flavor, and decided not to go home after all. Instead he decided to go across the street to the diner and murder some people. He wound his pickup truck dangerously across four lanes of traffic, taking out fences and guardrails as he did so. Horns blared and tires howled as oncoming vehicles desperately tried to avoid colliding with him. Leroy barely noticed. He brought the nearly ruined truck to a spitting, shuddering halt directly in front of the diner's front door, noticing without any real interest that everywhere people seemed to be engaged in some sort of conflict. Over by the phone booth two men were feeding each other knuckle sandwiches. In front of the exit two women were rolling around on the tarmac, pulling hair and screeching like banshees. There were more skirmishes in the back lot and several people had rammed their cars into other vehicles. One of them looked pretty bad. A man with blood on his face hung from an open window of a smashed vehicle while his wife stood by screaming for help. And beneath the lighted awning, in full view of everyone, a man's head came apart like it had contained an explosive charge. Leroy barely gave all of this carnage a second glance. He was a man with a mission. He grabbed his .357 magnum from the holster strapped beneath the seat, spun the cylinder and strode determinedly into the diner. Wow, was Fred Weir, the diner's owner, going to be surprised to see him. The son of a bitch would never make eyes at Wendy again. That was the truth.

CHAPTER ONE

Somewhere in the northern Maine wilderness, 8:30 am July, 7th. Three days after the arrival.

1

"I'm going out there," Doug told Annie. "I need to see what's happening." They were standing on the front porch of their small wilderness cabin staring across the clearing to the dark woods beyond as Ariel, their three year old daughter, stood at their feet clutching "Cabby" her tattered old Cabbage Patch doll—the one Rick Jennings had brought her when she was a year old—tightly to her bosom.

"Nothing's happening," Annie said. "The noise stopped three days ago."

Doug nodded thoughtfully. "My point exactly. Just about the time those guys paid us that visit."

"So you don't think it's just coincidence?" Annie said.

Doug shook his head. "Something's wrong and I need to find out what. I've waited long enough, maybe too long."

Annie hugged her arms to her body and glanced down at Ariel. "I don't want you to go, Doug. I almost lost you once. I can't go through that again."

Doug took Annie in his arms. He knew exactly what she was talking about. It had been a terrible time in their lives. There were moments when he believed he'd never see her again. There were moments when he believed Ariel would never be born. But so much had happened since. He looked down at the child and his heart swelled with love. She had made a believer out of him.

"You know I have to do this," he said.

Annie pushed away a little petulantly. Her face had deepened from fear to something worse, but she didn't say anything, only looked at him.

"We knew it couldn't last," he said. "We've gone over this how many times? We knew that eventually we'd have to resort to plan B."

"But we're not actually sure anything's wrong yet, are we?" There was a slight tone of hope in Annie's voice.

Doug kissed Annie on the nose. "Nope," he said trying to sound upbeat but not really feeling it. "But I need to make sure. What happened three nights ago has really been bugging me."

"But they went away."

"Yes, they went away. That's what bothers me. It doesn't make sense. They walked right through the outer perimeter but stayed well back from the inner one. Why do you think that is, Annie? It's almost like they were aware of the inner one . . . but hadn't yet gotten an update on the new one." He paused letting what he'd just said sink in.

"So, how do you think they knew?"

"I'm not saying they did. I'm just speculating. It seems fishy, that's all. Think about it. If they got that close, and it's the first time they've been here, then why did they go away? There has to be a reason."

Annie shivered. "So you're saying it might not be the first time they've been out there? That maybe they've been . . . watching us? Maybe they're just waiting for the right . . . moment?"

Doug did not reply. Annie had pretty much summed up his thoughts in a nutshell. He sat down and began determinedly lacing his boots. Afterward he went to the rack and took down his rifle, slung it over his shoulder, picked his two way radio up off the table, clipped it to his belt. "I just turned off the sensors," he said. "I'll key you when I get out beyond them. Turn them back on until you hear from me."

Annie nodded. Normally they turned the sensors off during the day, but since the incident the other night they'd been keeping both perimeters on twenty-four/seven.

"You know what to do if I . . ." He didn't finish the sentence because of course Annie knew exactly what to do and he didn't want to say it in front of Ariel. *If you lose contact with me and I don't come back within a "reasonable" time frame, get yourself and Ariel up to the ice caves and wait.*

Wait for what? Annie was thinking but she didn't say it. *Wait for Rick to come and save us, or wait for something else entirely? If I have to keep waiting I think I might go crazy.*

Annie also knew the rest of what she was supposed to do: *If anyone with harmful intent comes within range and I'm not around, then it's up to you to blow the perimeter. If that doesn't work and they somehow still get through, then set the cabin to blow and get Ariel up to the caves as fast as possible.*

This was the part that was hardest for Annie to accept. For the past almost four years the cabin had been their home, their lives, their only sanctuary. And she was supposed to just blow it up and destroy the only home—the only *life*—Ariel had ever known. Annie picked Ariel up and put on a brave face. Doug took them both in his arms in an extended bear hug.

Ariel clutched Cabby as if her life depended on it.

"I love you, Papa," Ariel said, kissing him on the cheek. "Cabby loves you too."

"Me too, Sunshine. You take care of your mother, okay?"

"I always will."

Together Annie and Ariel watched Doug cross the small clearing and disappear into the forest beyond.

"Papa's gone," Ariel said pointing after her father.

Annie shivered at Ariel's prophetic pronouncement.

"Only for a short while, Ariel," Annie said. "He'll be back."

"Maybe not this time," Ariel said, and a chill crawled the length of Annie's spine.

2

Out beyond the cabin, Doug assumed stealth mode, moving as quickly and as quietly as possible through the harsh environment that surrounded his world. He was careful not to use the same track he'd used last time or the time before that. In the three years since coming here he'd gotten very good at navigating his way through this rough and unforgiving land. He'd learned how to move without leaving a trail, how to track animals for food, and he'd become equally adept at locating errant humans who'd wandered too close to the compound for comfort. For several miles around the perimeter of the cabin he and Rick Jennings had installed motion detectors, and closer in: security cameras. Over the past three years a handful of hunters, hikers and just plain nosy had wandered into their space. Doug and Annie had always informed these interlopers, in the politest way possible, that this was private property and that they were not welcome here.

Suspicious, and increasingly uncomfortable with their situation, Doug had installed a new series of sensors out beyond the original perimeter. And just like that, it had been breached. It made him wonder how long they had been out there, out of sight, but so damned close. And if it was true, if they *were* out there watching them, what the hell were they waiting for? They knew Ariel was safe here. It's the only thing that made any sense. She was being nurtured by loving parents. She was too young to be of any use to them now. No, they would wait. And they would watch. And when they felt the time was right they would pounce.

The thought made Doug's blood run cold.

Three nights ago, when the outer perimeter detectors had gone off, Doug sat on the porch the remainder of that long night with his rifle across his lap and his finger on the inner perimeter detonator while Annie and Ariel slept soundly, unaware that anything was amiss. When dawn broke and all was quiet Doug struck off and found a series of fresh human tracks less than a quarter mile from the encampment. There were three separate sets of them, and on closer inspection he discovered that they'd been made with military-style combat boots. He followed them in a three hundred and sixty degree circumnavigation of the cabin. They had not ventured closer than the original quarter mile perimeter, as though they *were* aware of these limitations.

The unsettling thought had been eating at Doug ever since, that perhaps the feds had known where they were from the beginning. Jennings still worked as a law enforcement officer in Portland, and of course the feds had suspected from the beginning that he'd had something to do with Doug's and Annie's disappearance. Despite Rick's assurances Doug often wondered how hard it would be for them to learn what they needed to know. Rick made regular but infrequent trips carrying supplies into Parker Pond with his float plane. The feds weren't stupid.

Doug followed the trail until it disappeared in a small clearing at the foot of Stonewall Mountain five miles to the east. In the grass there he'd detected two long, straight indents that could only have been made by helicopter skids.

His heart sank. Coincidentally, or perhaps not so coincidental, it was the same day the noise had stopped. To Doug it felt like the world had taken a deep breath and was holding it. His instincts told him that something in the world had gone horribly awry. Something more than the fact that they'd been found. He wasn't sure what it was, but long ago he'd learned to trust his instincts. Surely their time here in the wilderness had come to an end and they needed to move on. After all they had been through, after all they'd fought for and sacrificed, they would never be safe no matter how far they ran. The thought depressed Doug. He was tired of running. Even more, he was tired of hiding.

The only light at the end of their long, dark tunnel was Ariel. In the years since her birth, she had become his and Annie's entire world. She was the most amazing child they'd ever known. He was aware that all parents thought that about their own child; it was natural, a built in mechanism that caused you to love and protect your own above all others. But Ariel *was* different. She had an aura about her that could not be denied. Almost four years had passed since her birth and she was talking like a child more than three times her age. Her IQ was off the charts. She was asking questions no child her age had a right to ask. She was intensely interested in all things scientific, from how the earth and its amazing array of living species happened, to the stars and planets in the night sky, wondering if there were others like us out there.

Rick had been flying books in for her and she had been devouring them like sustenance. Even so, her curiosity never waned. Doug and Annie had answered all her questions to the best of their abilities, but there was so much they didn't know. College and life experience had given them a reasonable amount of knowledge in many areas, but coming up with accurate answers to some of Ariel's amazing questions frustrated them both. And how much harder would the questions become as she grew older? They understood one thing clearly: there would come a time in the very near future when Ariel would need to draw on the wisdom of those much more learned than her parents.

The thought simultaneously scared Doug to death and gave him an intense sense of pride. How could he be the father of such an amazing child? How could he ever let her go? Sometimes late at night he'd come awake with a terrible fear inside him, growing, filling him up, until he was unsure if he had the strength to fight it. That's when he'd get out of bed and sit for a long time watching Annie and Ariel sleep. An overwhelming love would replace the fear when he realized what a gift they were. He *had* to be strong. They depended on him for survival and he would do anything to ensure their safety.

Even as he dreaded what the future was certain to hold, he knew deep in his heart that he would someday have to set Ariel free. Then who would protect her? There were those out there in the world who knew about her. They'd been aware of her since long before her birth, or even her conception. Some wanted to use her, some wanted to worship her, and some desperately wanted her gone from this earth. *If* she survived she would become a great prophet, she would inspire millions, and perhaps be the one with enough power and knowledge to lead humans up out of the cradle of their own civilization to the stars. Doug and Annie both knew there were those who would go to any length to control that power.

Regardless of her brilliance, Ariel was now still a

fragile little girl who needed to be protected. And Doug would protect her to his dying breath.

He hated leaving Annie and Ariel even for a few moments, but he needed to see for himself why the noise that had become so prevalent in their lives had stopped. Doug moved on toward the outer perimeter, every nerve in his body tense.

The silence was deafening. There was an edge to it that made his hackles rise. He didn't remember it ever being this quiet here. Not even before the machines had arrived.

3

For more than a year now the paper company had been harvesting timber beyond the perimeter of privately owned property around Parker Pond. Doug and Annie had gotten used to the distant rumbling of heavy machinery. Just the same, Doug didn't like the paper companies. In his eyes they were spoilers who raped the forest with impunity. They hauled the trees to the mill where they were ground into chips and mixed with chemicals to make wood mash which in turn was used to manufacture such things as newspapers, cardboard boxes and magazines. In the process, habitat for countless species of plant and animal was being destroyed, brooks and streams were warming and becoming unfit for native fish species, while rivers far downstream were polluted with dioxin. The companies that committed these crimes against nature were merciless. Everything and anything was justified in the quest for the almighty dollar. And there was nothing anyone could do about it. The paper companies owned the land and they could do whatever they wished with it.

In the past year or so Ariel had been waking in the night crying in anguish over the lives that were being lost because of the forest's destruction. When Doug and Annie had quizzed the child about what lives she was referring to she'd been unable to provide clear answers. "Just lives," she'd replied, and both parents had finally come to the conclusion that Ariel was referring to all life; trees, deer, moose, fish, cats, rodents and worms. Somehow she knew that every living species on earth was connected, and that all life had value. A realization that most humans never came to. Yet a three year old child had. Ariel wasn't just brilliant, she was ultra-sensitive, and Doug often wondered if she had some sort of direct psychic connection with nature.

He guessed that our status at the top of the food chain caused us to be arrogant in the face of these truths. Humans put themselves above all other life forms. Ariel knew instinctively that this was a mistake. Thanks to Ariel's keen intuition, Doug and Annie had become increasing more aware of these and other human crimes perpetrated against nature and wondered how much the planet could take before rebelling.

Finally, after more than a year, three days ago the far off but relentless sound of the machines had stopped. Just like that. And the sudden quiet was both a relief and a little unnerving.

And something else had happened at about the same time. Something they did not want to talk about because there was no rational explanation for it: when they turned on the radio, all they got was static. When they arrived here almost four years ago Doug and Rick had erected a small windmill in order to keep essential batteries charged. Atop the tower they had installed an AM/FM antenna. They were able to pick up a station in St. John, one in Millinocket, a few in Bangor, and on nights when atmospheric conditions were just right they could pick up a few FM stations from as far away as Portland and Boston. Now, no matter where they tuned the radio dial, all they got was static.

The tower was also equipped as a cell phone receiver/transmitter. Doug and Rick had installed it when they'd first come here, only to be used in case of emergency. They had all learned the hard way just how easy it was for those searching for signals to zero in on cell phones. The assumption was that cell towers were monitored for activity. There had been plenty of evidence of this over the past several years. The case of Edward Snowden for instance. He had exposed the government's penchant for monitoring cell phones as well as internet activity. Conversations were being listened to and analyzed. Homeland Security had computer programs with sophisticated software. Individual words could trigger alerts. Doug, Rick and Annie had all agreed that the phone would be used only if absolutely necessary. After the incident the other night they'd broken protocol and tried calling Rick Jennings.

They hadn't gotten as much as a dial tone.

It was as if there was no longer an outgoing signal. Doug had tested all the settings on the tower and they all seemed to be working correctly. The disquieting thought struck him that perhaps the problem wasn't on his end.

Before reaching the cutoff Doug keyed the transmitter on his two-way. "Annie, can you hear me?"

A moment of static was followed by Annie's voice. "Loud and clear."

"You can turn the sensors back on."

"Done. How are things?"

"So far, so good. I'll give you an update when I reach the cutoff."

"Be careful, Doug."

"Will do. Over and out."

4

Once he reached the edge of the forest where it met the massive cutoff Doug stopped and stood very still watching for movement. Nothing stirred. Not even the leaves on the trees. It occurred to him that he hadn't seen so much as a rabbit or a squirrel all morning. The preternatural silence, coupled with the forest's stillness, was like an omen, giving him pause, making him stand and gaze out over the cut longer than he should have.

The road down through the cutoff was littered with trucks, mostly late models, most of them four wheel drives with North Woods Timber stenciled on the doors. All sat motionless. The huge tree harvesters all stood motionless as well. They looked like the calcified remains of some alien Transformer species.

Rarely did he stray this far from the compound, and he would never voluntarily expose his presence to these forest workers, although he was quite certain they knew about them. Were any of them out there watching him now, wondering who this strange person with camouflage clothing and the slung rifle was? From what he could see, he doubted it. He almost wished they *were* there. Perhaps the sight of another living human would help to ease the tension building in him.

But Doug saw no human activity.

And heard no noise.

This was all wrong. If their work here was done then the machines should have been gone.

Doug surveyed the road beyond the motionless vehicles. It was made of dirt and stone, and ran in a convolution of perhaps ten miles down through the barren cut where forest had once stood. Purple sawtooth mountains that hadn't been visible when they'd first come here now broke the distant horizon.

Doug remained very still, breathing in, and breathing out. The smell of gasoline and burnt motor oil and hydraulic fluid drifted across the cut and mixed with the dead smells of dust, rot and old wood.

He trained his eyes skyward. He'd gotten used to the contrails of jetliners high up in the atmosphere as they flew their routes between Europe and the U.S. and back again. Though the sky was clean and blue and cloudless, he saw no contrails. He hadn't seen a contrail in days.

Finally Doug left his vantage at the edge of the forest and carefully worked his way out into the cut toward the motionless vehicles. Cautiously he approached the closest vehicle to him, a forest green Ford F-250 with the driver side door standing wide open. He leaned around the open door and peered into the cab. It was empty, and although the door was open the dome light was not lit. Doug saw that the ignition key was turned to the ON position. He reached in and turned it to start. The starter clicked. Once. Twice. Then died.

No life left in the battery. This truck had been sitting here with the door open for quite some time.

He moved cautiously along the road until he came to another vehicle. It too sat empty. As did the next. The fourth vehicle was a Grapple Yarder, a giant of a vehicle with tracks like a tank and a long articulated arm with a grapple hook attached to the end. This particular machine was designed to stack logs along the sides of roads, and later to load them into the beds of trucks.

Doug inched cautiously closer to the vehicle. Like the first pickup truck the door stood open. A man without a head hung from the cab.

5

Doug backed carefully away, turned and began sprinting back toward the woods.

A distant buzz-saw sound made him stop.

At first he could not identify it, but as the noise grew louder, and closer, instinctively, he understood what he was hearing.

He plucked the two-way radio off his belt and keyed the button as he resumed his run toward the perimeter. "Annie! Get away from the cabin now!" he cried through grunts of exertion.

Static sounded and Annie's voice came back to him. "What's wrong?"

"Don't ask questions. Just do it, now! Take Ariel and run as fast as you can to the caves. Don't stop and don't look back. I'll meet you there. Go! Now!"

"We're on our way," Annie's breathless voice answered back and Doug knew she was running.

Doug was close to the perimeter of trees now, his powerful legs pumping like pistons. He pulled his weapon from around his neck and jacked a round into the chamber. He made the perimeter just as the large Predator Drone screamed over his head. A moment later twin missiles fired from the drone's undercarriage followed by a series of powerful explosions that shook the earth and staggered him. In the distance a small mushroom cloud rose above the trees.

Doug stopped, his breath coming in massive spasms. He could not believe his eyes. Horrified, he stood and watched smoke and fire belch above the forest.

The cabin had been destroyed.

In the next instant the inner perimeter detonated, a

three hundred and sixty degree circle of fiery staccato blasts that lifted Doug off his feet and blew him ten feet back from where he'd been standing. He came down hard on his back, the wind punched from his lungs. He lay breathing in spasms feeling like his lungs had been flash fried. He did a quick pat down of his body to make sure he wasn't on fire. He wasn't.

Even as Doug struggled to his feet, he heard the drone's engines whine above the crackling sound of the burning forest, and knew that it was banking back around for another go. Doug pictured a room with a technician/pilot sitting behind a console directing the drone's flight path. Behind him stood members of a shadow government ordering his every move.

Was it possible that he'd been seen? Was the drone retracing its flight path so that it could fire at *him*, or had it spotted Annie and Ariel making their way up toward the ice caves? He prayed that they'd heard the explosions and had taken cover until the drone had passed overhead.

Either way the drone must not be allowed to unleash any more hellfire. Doug's weapon was an AR-15 assault rifle with a fully automatic function. He snapped the switch to automatic. Up ahead there was a small clearing. He sprinted towards it hoping for a shot unencumbered by tree tops. The drone was gaining fast, however, looping back around and taking the same path as before. He knew he was vulnerable standing out in the open. But he did not care. Annie and Ariel must be protected at all costs. He faced the direction of the oncoming drone aiming his weapon skyward. As it approached, the drone unleashed a volley of .50 Caliber rounds which churned up the forest in their haste to reach the small clearing in which

Doug stood.

He had been seen. There was no doubt about it.

Doug aimed his weapon skyward and placed the sight directly on the nose of the screeching drone. Not waiting for the aircraft to get any closer he depressed the trigger. In fully automatic mode the AR-15 fires at the rate of 800 rounds per minute. As the weapon hammered his sore shoulder Doug drew the sight along a straight line just ahead of the drone's flight path, and then lifting the barrel higher and faster, he spread the line of fire out ahead of the drone. In theory the drone would fly directly into his volley.

Doug stood his ground even as the .50 caliber rounds spitting from the drone inched ever closer, chewing off the tops off trees and tearing up the forest floor. In a matter of seconds the rounds would strafe the clearing and cut him down.

Still Doug did not move. He would fire until the rifle's magazine was empty.

A sudden explosion rocked the drone, its left side sagging, sending its .50 caliber rounds flying wildly off into the forest. The drone began to tumble, a fiery pinwheel rolling toward the earth on a trajectory directly toward the clearing in which Doug stood.

He did not wait around to see what would happen but exploded into a run. He'd made perhaps fifty yards when the drone struck the earth, erupting in a singeing burst of orange fire. A second later a dull boom rolled across the forest on a pressure wave strong enough to stagger him and knock him to his knees.

Doug felt heat on his back and smelled hair burning as he scratched his way to his feet and kept running. He did not venture a glance back, but kept moving in the direction of the cabin, through the perimeter of diminishing flame, his hand reaching for the two-way radio on his belt.

23